THE SECRET NAMES
OF WOMEN

Books by Lynne Barrett

The Land of Go
The Secret Names of Women

as editor
(with Roy Hoopes)
The James M. Cain Cookbook

THE SECRET NAMES
OF WOMEN

STORIES BY

LYNNE BARRETT

CARNEGIE MELLON UNIVERSITY PRESS
PITTSBURGH 1999

ACKNOWLEDGMENTS

The author is grateful for permission to reprint stories that originally appeared, sometimes in different form, in the following publications: *Ellery Queen's Mystery Magazine* ("Elvis Lives"), *Marilyn: Shades of Blonde* ("Hush Money"), *Mondo Barbie* ("Beauty"), *Other Voices* ("Macy Is The Other Woman"), and *Tampa Review* ("To Go").

⚜

This book was completed with the assistance of a fellowship from the National Endowment for the Arts.

⚜

Thanks to David Beaty, Marguerite Beaty, Tracey Broussard, Rebecca Callahan, Jason Gibbs, The Gourmet Diner, Robert Gregory, Pamela Gross, Dennis Lehane, Kat Meads, Charles Radke, Dena Santoro, Weslea Sidon, and Virginia Wells for their help and support. And thanks, most of all, to Bob and James.

ß

Book Design: Nancy Ramsey

CONTENTS

Friends of Carnegie Mellon University Press

The publisher wishes to acknowledge the following Series in Short Fiction benefactors:

Sally Levin, David Baker, Mort and Rita Seltman, Ellen and Greg Kander, Lou and Amy Weiss, Sabina Deitrick, Vit and Bernie Friedman, Susan Golomb, Megan Gayle, Vera Moore, Eleanor and Bruce Feldman, Walnut Capital Management, Marilyn and Earl Latterman, Mr. and Mrs. Jeffery Cohen, Jack and Andy Weiss, Rich Engel, Jen Bannan, Cathy Lewis, Steve Leper, Jim Daniels, Kristen Kovacic, Pat and Bob Gorzyca, Gretchen A. McBeath, David Lewis, Robert Morison, Caliban Book Shop, Susan and Steve Zelicoff, Gerald Costanzo.

FOR R.F.M.

TO GO

So I insist that we stop and at least I'll get something to go, even if B.K. won't come in, won't eat, his stomach nervous, he's in such a rush to make Clewiston by noon. He stays in the cool car

while I pass through bright heat into one of those places, lunch counter/souvenir store, where the air has the sweet mustiness of pecans and orange wine. I wait while they zap the sausage biscuits and when I come out with iced teas on a tray and hop into the Chrysler

he's dead. Hunched over the wheel with the same glare he had when he drove a two-lane and some old-timer in an Air Stream got ahead of him and nothing, not flashing the highbeams, not honking, not gunning up to ride three inches from the guy's bumper, nothing would make the slow poke speed up. B.K. looks just like that now, aggravated

and dead, clutching the wheel. His cheeks are slippery with tears and there's a faint bad smell. The air conditioner is blasting. The motor runs ragged. I stick my foot over and press his shoe down on the gas and the idle richens. I want to charge inside and howl for help, but I know for once in my life I ought to stop and think. I look out through purple tinted windows at the parking lot—nobody in sight but some family at a picnic table under the big sign for LIVE BABY ALLIGATORS and GOAT'S MILK FUDGE. If I go inside I'll have to say

Excuse me, Mr. Brian Kittery is out there, dead. It must have been his heart. His stomach bothered him last night, but it always did. He used to say, "Nobody dies of indigestion." And it never slowed him down. Sure, we did it last night, me leaning on the motel table, looking out the window at the moonlit swimming pool, him with his pants around his ankles as if when he finished he would yank them up and dash—but that was his favorite way and it was his idea, don't blame me,

he wouldn't, he wasn't that kind of guy. Impatient, sure, with inept cashiers, Zavala Junior in the Home Office, but basically fair. He groused about phoning his wife in Arcadia every evening at seven, but he called her on the dot, I noticed. When I first rode with him, six weeks ago, he was so jumpy I thought he could be one of those guys like they show on TV, Mr. Normal Church Choir Wife and Two Kids in Little League, who is socking it away the whole time, stealing everyone's investments, and then takes off— but no, I got to see he was just in a rush, horny, in hock, buying scratch-off lottery tickets, pressing to make time on the road, driving

up and down Florida stopping in every I Love Jesus Beauty Parlor & Auto Repair to sell his line of beauty products—Seagrape Scrub and Alligator Mask and Key Lime Conditioner, with me as his demo. It was his great idea, my fake i.d. saying I'm 42 years old and look 30, when really I'm 26 looking 30, which is an achievement if you ask me because I've been through enough to look 42. We like to say life is short

but it's a long long time when you're sitting in it. When I met him, I was in Cocoa, doing a Miller Lite promotion, giving out free hats in a sports lounge during Monday Night Football, wearing short shorts and high heels. "Nice wheels," he said, meaning my legs. I told him I taught aerobics in the daytime, was saving for a move to Miami, where you can get work as a dancer, and he said, "Why wait?" Big man, seventeen inch neck, eating chicken fingers. That night we got as far as Briny Breezes, Palm Beach County, and next morning, just for me, he took the slow route down the A1A past the oceanfront millionaire houses, to Miami. While he stopped at the Home Office, Señora Zavala's storefront in Coconut

Grove, I checked out the rents and decided to say yes to a swing around the state with him, zigzagging: Naples-Fort Pierce-Tampa-Orlando-Daytona-Jacksonville and then the long glide out the Panhandle where I saw my granny. And then back down, opening up new territory. Amazing how fast the state changes, new cutteries in strip malls and vanished salons. From one month to the next he lost three shops in Okeechobee. Florida is motion

even on this part of 27, the old tourist trail through orange country, it's eleven in the morning and the parking lot is beginning to fill up for lunch. Nobody gives us a glance, but I think it'll look better if we seem to be eating, so I stick a straw in my tea and suck its sweetness, chew the warm fat of my sausage biscuit while I try to figure out my situation. I keep looking at his eyes, dark blue with the long lashes of a loverboy. Reassuring shoulders. I liked him. He'd say,

"Make your own luck," he believed in hard work and drive, but who's gonna stand up at the funeral and say, At least he made those last three calls. Honestly, what'll happen if I go, Excuse me, this man is dead. No, I had no warning, Sheriff—

they have sheriffs, places like this, elected for their swagger and intolerance of strangers—

Well, I didn't really know him and um. Can't say my boyfriend. My employer, and please call his dear wife. She must suspect he was out here with someone like me, though women, my God, women can not-know whatever they put their minds to. Turn him into a shadow and concentrate on the kids. Then she'll be here and Zavala Junior will say B.K. was supposed to do his demo on a local girl each time and when they check the motel records they'll know we slept together if you can call it sleep, him always on the side nearest the door, grinding his teeth. Something was chasing him and I guess it's caught him now. He won't be resting any easier if there's a fuss. Excuse me, I noticed this man in a parked car, he hasn't moved, I think he's dead. How did I get here, though? Excuse me, I was just hitchhiking. Excuse me, Sheriff—and then I better not have i.d. for Carrie Hull, 42. B.K. got her birth certificate, a little girl he went to school with who died, leukemia. He must've liked her all those years ago, he said it was like we were giving her another chance, but that driver's license with my picture, my granny's address, is fraud, probably a felony. How simple it was when I used to be

Ruth Ann Reedy, just a little cracker girl from Paxton, highest point in Florida, 345 feet, right near the Alabama line. And then Ruth Ann Wheeler when I married at 19. Jeep Wheeler threatened me into it and I was fool enough to think if I gave in he'd be reassured and uncrazy. On our honeymoon weekend in St. Pete he punched me out so, duh, I wised up. Back in Paxton went to a lawyer and said, "You'll think I'm weird, I've been married five days and I want a divorce," and the lawyer said, "Happens all the time." When I was hiding out, then, Jeep beat his mother up, and she got me word to come sign the papers to commit him for observation, which I did. Before he could get loose

I took off, went back to Reedy, made it Reed, and cocktail waitressed and studied dance in Tampa, where they started calling me Ginger in tap class. It's Ginger Reed with the record for disturbing the peace, cause when I drank rum I liked to do the time step, *flap shuffle flap shuffle flap ball change*, on the roof of my apartment building. And it's Ginger Reed who got pulled in when they raided the exotic dance club in Daytona where I was shaking it for the college boys. Charges dropped but those sheriffs can still get in to where it's on record and Now then little lady, you've got quite a past, they say while they're checking out your boobs. Which makes me think this leotard, fine for demonstrating Avocado Bosom Cream, shows too much for any decent Excuse Me's

so I recline the passenger seat and slither through to crouch under B.K.'s suits and shirts hanging from the rack across the back seat. I wriggle into a long cotton skirt and t-shirt, switch my silver sandals for my Keds. I take down the two dresses I'd hung up, stuff everything in my big soft bag. Check to make sure my money's in my tampon box, the place I figure no thief will look. I guess I can't take the sample case, so I just snag some Orange Mint Restorer, Señora Zavala's original recipe, cause I really think it's done my skin a lot of good. I toss my bag up front and when I get in the seat and slowly crank it up I see

an old school bus, painted blue, has pulled into the lot. Home-
made script proclaims Christ's Canaries, Choir of the First Church
of Our Savior Sanctified. Out come round-faced women with vir-
tuous perms. They look like home to me. Excuse me, but some
sinning fellow ditched me here and could you please give me a lift?
Excuse me, I'm working my way to my granny's in Sebring,
Clewiston, wherever you're going. I'll mingle with them in the
bathroom line. I'm a second soprano, Carrie Hull, age 42—why,
thank you, if I look good it must be living clean. B.K. will get
found on his own. They'll shut down for the night and there he'll
be, car stalled, heart attack, and no one will even know I was here.
I gather our food wraps and get out, soft bag across my shoulder,
purse in hand. At the trash basket I turn,

look at him across the parking lot. He stares into the tinted
windshield like any man left waiting for a woman. He must hate
being stuck. He used to take right turns on red just to keep moving. We'd twine through a town not yet on the map and he'd grin
when I worried and say, "We may be lost, but we're making good
time."

HUSH MONEY

My name is Annie O'Malley. You may have seen my work behind the famous as they relax in their gardens in *People* or *In Style*—that's what I do, I'm gardener to the stars. My profession requires me to live with secrets. This isn't so easy—a secret can be poison, burning in your mouth till you have to spit it out. I sometimes think that's really what motivates those who tattle to the tabloids, more than money or attention. My solution has been to write things down. I tell myself that I want the truth to be known someday, that I'm interested in justice, but mostly I just need to spill the beans.

❦

I'd only been in Hollywood for a year or so. I'd finished the all-green garden of the producer Paul Ferris and moved on to land-scaping the place of Jill Santiago, an ex-girlfriend of his. His ex-girlfriends were all fond of him, they formed a regular club, and in a way I was a member of it, too, so they were each in turn hiring me. Jill had begun as a starlet in adventure films, had failed in a couple of more serious flicks, and now, having decided to get rich, was a sensational bitch on a nighttime soap. She had honed her figure into an instrument with which she tortured men, something it turns out women enjoy watching.

In person Jill was a combination of pragmatic and crazy that is quite common out here. She was happy with me because I had succeeded in moving into her yard an espaliered wisteria complete with its very nice old wall that went back to the Spanish settlement of California and cost a fortune, but the point was that Jill needed the wisteria to look as if it had been there behind her house (built in 1986) for generations and to bloom in just the shade she wanted behind her when Barbara Walters interviewed her. This had gone off perfectly. She looked gorgeous as they talked, her hair baby blond against the lavender blue wisteria, and Barbara had been so mellowed out by the breeze and blossoms that she didn't press Jill on the rumors that her body was surgically contrived. Somehow the old Spanish wall vouched for Jill's genuineness.

Jill cheerfully paid the bill for the crew and equipment I'd used, said I was a genius, and gave me the assignment of going up to this property in Northern California she'd bought. Her accountant said she needed to use the place, and it was up to me to decide how. "Not grapes," she said, "grapes take too long. I heard from Paul that that vineyard of his won't produce anything worth drinking for seven years. Coolidge (the acountant) says it would be good if I took some losses as write-offs—but I'd rather see a profit. I want a business hobby. It should be intelligent, feminine, unusual—but do-able."

"A lot of people are raising exotic animals," I told her. "Ostriches or giraffes."

"Animals steal scenes. Think of a good plant," she said, "in my color range of course."

You may think this was an idiotic assignment, but I found it amusing. That's what it takes, I guess, to be gardener to the stars.

✻

The property was not far from Geyserville, in Lake County. Late in the afternoon I came up a twisting road in the car I had rented in San Francisco, admiring old estates and picturesque shacks, roadsides bright with poppies and fields planted in tight rows of grapevines, just sprouting in early April. The road wound nauseatingly along a ridge and after I passed a funny encampment of pink cottages at the peak, it plunged down and died out. You could see the trail beyond it where the road had once continued, but it was overgrown and flinty, so I decided I'd need four wheel drive to take it on. I went back uphill to the pink cottages and parked under a vast hedge of rosemary, thinking I'd ask if there was another way in. The cottages, four of them, formed a rough quad around a fragrant garden. I knocked on the blue front door of the biggest house and waited, admiring the generous patches of lavender and thrift. I was squatting before columbines in blossom, when a gruff and rusty voice behind me said, "Get the hell out of here."

I turned and saw an old lady, tall and tanned to leather, wearing many silver bracelets and a purple bath towel. Her white hair was pulled up in a big purple clip and her legs were wet. Behind her water dripped from what I realized was an outdoor shower closed in by lattice overgrown with wild pink roses.

"I'm terribly sorry," I said. "I'm trying to get over to the next property, over there. The owner sent me to—"

"It got sold again?"

I nodded. "The owner is Jill Santiago and she sent me up to look it over, see what it needs." I handed her my card.

She looked it over. "L.A." Her laugh was a caw. "People in L.A. have been selling that property to each other for forty years," she said.

"What happened to the road?"

"Flooded out. That road extended right across a streambed, joins up with the creek down there. Floods every ten years or so. Last couple of times nobody came in to rebuild it—nobody complained. I sure didn't."

Though her voice was rough and her stance unfriendly, I admired her. How magnificent to be an old lady living out here, I thought, showering among the roses. She was a vision of the kind of old woman I'd like to be someday.

"I'm sorry to have intruded," I said. "You'll be seeing me go through here, but I'll try not to disturb you again."

"I'm sure," she sighed, "this is only the beginning of disturbances."

"I'm sorry," I said again, and turned to go back to my car.

But she said, "Come on in," and led me into the cottage with the blue door. The main room was a kitchen, and she said to me, "Hang on," and went into another room for a moment. I waited, mildly confused at the shift into friendliness—if it was friendliness. She came back in a long yellow Mexican dress. "You must forgive me," she said. "I'm out of practice seeing people. Mostly it's just the men who come to work on the grapes. I lease the vines to a winery down the valley—Mea Vinca, you ever have that wine? That's got some of my grapes in it. I get cases of it, free. Want some?"

"Huh?"

"Want some wine?"

I nodded. She went to a green painted sideboard and brought out a bottle and green chunky glasses and poured us each a good slug. I drank, standing, not really certain of my welcome. She stood too.

"So you work in L.A.," she said. "I used to live there. During the war and right after."

"Long time ago," I said.

"Oh, I'm sure it's the same," she said. "Underneath the surface, not much really changes. L.A. is a place full of cannibals. Well, all of California, really. You know about the Donner party? Cannibalism founded California and cannibals we remain," she said.

"That's harsh," I said.

"Where are you from?"

"Massachusetts."

"You'll learn," she said. "Maybe you're already learning." She laughed—that caw again— "I learned, but it took me a few years. I knew Marilyn Monroe."

"Really? Well—I guess she got eaten up all right. I see what you mean."

"Hah," she barked. " I doubt you do."

"How did you know her?"

"See," she said, "you're hungry too. You want to taste that stardust."

I must have looked confused—I wasn't sure if I should be amused or offended. I swallowed my wine—a fiercely tannic cabernet—and started moving to the door. "Well, I thank you very much for the drink. You'll see me going by."

She reached out and shook my hand. "I'm Mrs. Donofrio," she said. "Forgive me if I startled you. Like I said, I don't see so many people. When my husband was alive we had more company."

I left and when I got in my car said *Whew*. On the way back down the ridge I saw that quite a bit of what must be her land was planted with grapevines, their rows of T-shaped trellises oddly geometric in contrast to the hodgepodge of her cottages and garden.

I drove back into Geyserville, where I'd arranged to stay in a bed and breakfast. I asked about Mrs. Donofrio, but the owners didn't know much—they'd bought the B & B only a few months before, moving up to flee L.A. My host told me tales of the people living in the inaccessible spots here, old hippies who'd stayed on, pot farmers, people who liked to be beyond easy reach of the law. He told me I was lucky nobody'd taken a shot at me. But somehow none of these stories fit my old woman. She had seemed awkwardly friendly, lonely. I studied a county map they had and saw a stream bed that marked the line between the properties. I had to call over to Calistoga to make arrangements to swap my rental car for a jeep next day.

※

This time I was able to get down the hill and across and I walked all over the property. There was a tumble-down house—turn of the century it looked, the ghost of a white villa. The land was hillside meadow, full of lupine and campanula and other wildflowers I didn't recognize. Old unpruned lilacs were in bloom and there was a dark blue hedge I knew Jill would like—some kind of heather. At lunchtime I had a picnic with some sandwiches and Calistoga water I'd brought and realized that I could spy on the old lady of the pink cottages. She kept busy. She repainted some blue window boxes and then dug out what I imagined would be a vegetable patch.

The woman had a smooth, easy motion with a shovel. Watching her work made me feel lazy and I leaned back and went into a kind of doze, wondering what I was going to tell Jill to do with this place. The house could be beautiful if someone put in a lot of time and money, but I couldn't imagine Jill coming to live here—too far from everyone who mattered to her. And the logical thing to plant was grapes, but she had already nixed that. I felt reluctant to plant the place up with something she didn't really care about, something that would only get neglected again after her need for a hobby to display had been satisfied. I thought about Mrs. Donofrio's cannibals and I'm afraid got into a very unpleasant dream about several famous people threatening me with knives.

When I woke up I felt headachy—I'm a bad napper—and decided to pack it in for the day. But as I jounced across the streambed, I saw Mrs. Donofrio up ahead, waiting for me. Who's going to disturb who here, I thought, but I pulled up beside her.

I declined her offer of wine—said my head hurt—and she said she had an herbal tea that would help. I was curious about her life up here, so I said sure and let her lead me into the east cottage, which was a reading room, with redwood shelves floor to ceiling and a comfortable-looking couch covered by an old quilt. She went over to a side table, where she had an electric kettle, and while she made my tea I walked around exclaiming over the hundreds of books.

"Erle Stanley Gardner camped over there on your boss's land at one time. You know he used to go around California in his camper. Travelled with his girl secretaries—a couple of 'em. Dictated three books at once, they said. We liked him, my husband and I. My husband collected all his books. I guess that's what got us started." She showed me the shelves of Erle Stanley Gardner—paperbacks with lurid covers. The ones from the forties might have been valuable, but they were just stacked up, not displayed. I moved along, noticing sets of Stevenson and Twain, encyclopedias, some dinged-up science texts. Then I reached a shelf of old gardening books that made my mouth water. She had volumes of Jepson's *A Flora of California* and a gilt-edged Gertrude Jekyll from 1904, *Old West Surrey*, that goes for $250 if you can ever find it. I started talking about them—babbling—and saw she was listening to me amusedly. "Maybe you'd like to borrow one or two of these," she said.

I took the Gertrude Jekyll—determined to photocopy every page of it—and a book on California wildflowers. While her rosemary tea cleared my head, she told me how she'd never had much education but once she lived up here she'd started reading. I noticed that though her voice was gruff and low there was a music to it I liked.

✼

In the days that passed I got in the habit of stopping by at the end of the day. I'd identified monkshood and shooting star and seven shades of nemophilas. I made a map and sat on Jill's land reading books and making plans—she could raise roses, I thought one day—maybe she should make a country garden, I thought the next. I made sketch after sketch, but nothing satisfied me. After this I would stop at Mrs. Donofrio's and we would have a glass of wine. I showed her some of the wildflowers I'd sketched and she told me how the Indians had used blue curls for medicine and once went to war to drive settlers off their fields of camas, the wild hyacinth whose bulbs they ate in ceremonies. I told her a few tales of Hollywood—she liked the one about the old man I'd met who was one of the gardeners that planted and tended a thousand Scottish heather plants for Samuel Goldwyn's *Wuthering Heights*. But she didn't again mention Marilyn Monroe.

Then the winery men came one day. They appeared to be doing some careful pruning. I saw them taking turns going into her bathroom and spreading their lunch at a table outside. Mrs. Donofrio didn't come out. I was doing soil tests—using my pH kit, sampling and labelling. It was precise work and I nearly jumped when someone cleared her throat and I saw Mrs. Donofrio sitting above me on a jag of rock.

I looked over at the men. "Did they drive you away?"

She shrugged. "You get used to the quiet."

"What are they doing?"

"Oh, it's all a science now—they have systems for arranging every leaf to get the most sun and air. Not the way it was when I first came up here, when the old men from Italy tended the vines."

"Well, I'm sure they were trying to wring as much as they could out of nature, too."

"You're a nice girl," she said. "I think you should leave Los Angeles."

"Actually I can't," I said. And I told her some personal things, how I came out to look after my sister in the first place but then lucked into this work. Back East, without the graduate degree or connections to get hired at one of the big botanical gardens, I had just labored for landscapers. Now I felt I'd pulled something off getting these Hollywood people to pay for my garden dreams.

Maybe I even told her who I was carrying the torch for. The point is, I offered her some secrets of mine.

"I see," Mrs. D said. She sat with her arms clasped around her knees, like a young girl, looking across at her own home. "My first name is Wanita," she said. Her voice hit a rusty patch just then so I got the idea she hadn't spoken her own name in quite a while.

"Juanita's a beautiful name."

"W-a-n," she said. "My mother heard it in a song but she didn't know how to spell it. They were Okies, my people, trekked out here, didn't know a Spanish soul then. Wanita. Maybe the exotic name is what put it in my head to go to L.A."

"Where were you living?"

"I grew up near Sacramento. I was a big girl always, tall, with large hands and feet. Not beautiful—no, I had no illusions about that. Still, I had something going for me. Men paid attention to me. But this was during the war, there weren't so many men around. I thought I could do better in L.A." She gave her harsh laugh. "And maybe I thought someone would discover me, doll me up and put me in the movies. Sure.

"I was eighteen when I got there, in 1944. I fell in love right away with a sailor who was about to ship out. Jimmy Blue Eyes, I called him—I guess he reminded me of Frank Sinatra. Before the war he'd been a salesman—sewing machines, mainly—and he'd travelled all over the state. He talked about coming up here someday, to run some tourist cabins, maybe to farm. He wanted to marry me, but he said it wasn't fair to do that to me and then ship out and get killed. So he left me in L.A., and he didn't expect me to be a good girl, and I wasn't.

"I dated a lot of men—soldiers, sailors, four-flushers. Hollywood was loaded with four-flushers. What? Oh, a four-flusher was 4F, bad lungs, flat feet, some bit of him disabled him for war. Not that you could tell—big strapping handsome men there were who couldn't go to war, while my Jimmy Blue Eyes was a skinny guy, but he was in the Pacific on a destroyer.

"Early in the summer of '45 I met Norma Jean. I was in a gambling club in Santa Monica—a night on the town with some fella—Hal? Harry? No, I don't remember his name. Anyway, she was a pretty girl, no question about it. Not as beautiful as she was later. That was something I noticed about her—she got more beautiful all the time—I could see that even in a matter of weeks. Later, people said she had surgery on her nose, but there are things you can't get by cutting. She had a lovely smile. And she had wonderful feet—I must have noticed that because my own were big and boney. You didn't often see a girl with pretty feet—back then we all squeezed into too-small shoes and ruined them. Vanity. Hers stayed nice—you can see her feet in those late pictures where she's naked in a swimming pool. I've often wondered about her feet, how they stayed beautiful—silly I guess.

"Her date knew mine and so we gambled—or they did and we clung to their arms—and we went off to the powder room together. You probably don't know what powder rooms were like back then. The clubs had attendants in uniforms and an array of anything you might need for repairs to your dress or your face. We carried just these little clutch bags because we knew we could get help anywhere along the way—at dinner, nightclub, gambling house. I see you young women dragging those shoulder bags and I laugh.

"Norma Jean seemed real insecure. I remember she chattered even while she tinkled in the stall next to mine—" At my expression Wanita roared with laughter. "'I pissed with Marilyn Monroe.' I can see you don't really believe in the humanness of these people. But in your line of work you ought to know. You'll get to know. Anyway, 'Do you think he really likes me?' she said, and I noticed she stuttered a little. Real insecure. I tried to reassure her and when we came out and let the attendant brush us up a bit she said, 'I can tell your guy is crazy about you. You know just how to talk to him.'

"Don't look surprised. It was true. I spoke to men with respectful sweetness. I had doted on my dad, I guess that's why. But on top of that I'd been having elocution lessons, trying to get the Okie out of my voice, so I was flattered by her. I figured I must sound real proper." She laughed and shook her head.

"When we got back to the table my date was winning big and after he ran up a good sum we quit and went dancing with Norma Jean and her date. Her date was a good-looking boy. Mine was kind of an ordinary guy, maybe a little dull, but winning brightened him up and he bought us all a late dinner and next day he sent over this bracelet here—" She showed me a silver piece with green stones carved into Aztec faces, one of the heaviest she wore. "I started collecting these then. I liked Mexican jewelry—thought it went with my name. Norma Jean was at my place when it arrived. She'd called me and come over early, when I was still in bed, and we sat around and had some toast and talked. I had a swell little apartment. In Hollywood then they had buildings that were really swank. Downstairs there'd be a lobby like a hotel's and no one came up without asking at the desk. Your phone was on a switchboard. It was a nice place, hard to come by in the war, but a gentleman I knew owned the building."

Here Wanita went off into space for a minute, thinking, I supposed, about the man who owned the building, so I asked her what she and Norma Jean had talked about that day.

"This and that. I learned she was married but planning to divorce the fellow, who was overseas. She was doing some modelling and trying to study acting, living a life much like mine, working a bit and mooching off men to get by.

"Anyway, Norma Jean was a fun girl and she gave me a rush—invited me to the beach, I recall, and set up several double dates.

When we were on our own she was *so* interested in me—made me tell long stories about growing up in the Sacramento Valley and how I came to L.A. and all my adventures while I waited for Jimmy Blue Eyes. Even I thought they weren't that fascinating, but she would listen, all attention. By then I thought she was my best friend. I remember her curled up on the day bed I had filled with pillows in pretty textiles. She had light brown curly hair then and wore a little sundress with red bobbles on it that I liked—oh, she was a picture. I had told her about Jimmy Blue Eyes and our dream of coming up here after the war, if he would only live that long, and I must have expressed some confusion about loving him and going out with all these fellows, because she said, 'You can't help it, can you?'

"And I was touched that she understood. 'No, honey, I really can't,' I said. 'I see these men and they're just so appreciative, you know, and—' We didn't have such good words for sexy things then. Later, I'd have said they turned me on, but in the forties I said, 'They get to me,' and Norma nodded.

"She had told me herself that she wasn't so interested in sex as in ambition. She wanted to be an actress. She talked about her mother, the woman she didn't want to be—deserted, pathetic, nuts. And she told me about the actresses she'd seen when she was a girl, when her mother worked at a film lab. There was one actress whose walk she said she'd practiced—not somebody famous—she was not that pretty maybe, or maybe she got in trouble with a man, I forget, but Norma Jean said she had a sensational walk. Norma Jean described how she'd practiced it, when she was still just nine or ten. I wish I could recall her name now. Nobody you'd have heard of.

"Hey," Wanita said. "Let's have some dinner."

I was surprised to realize the sun had dropped. I'd been off in the forties with Wanita and Norma Jean. The men who'd been working on the vines were gone.

I gathered my things and drove her back over to her place. She sent me into her garden to pick arugula and sorrel for a salad. She blendered a gazpacho and grilled some salmon. "Fish and raw stuff," Wanita said, "that's the secret to long life. And wine."

We talked for a while about Jill's land and what might be done with it. I was anxious to assure her that whatever it would be wouldn't interfere with her too much, but Wanita just shook her head.

"I'll be watching reporters chase her, before you're through. I can tell she's a cannibal princess."

"Well, it won't last long," I said.

Wanita smiled. "Their fancy moves on."

"What about Norma Jean?" I asked. "Was that the whole story?"

"No, not quite. If I tell you," she said, "you'd have to keep the secret."

"I'm good at keeping secrets," I said. Well, I thought I was.

"Maybe it might help you out, in your work, help you to understand."

I tried to look receptive, ready to learn. We went out on the lawn and sat in old metal lawnchairs, eating fresh figs and goat cheese, drinking more wine. As darkness fell I could hardly see Wanita, just hear her. Her voice had warmed up—I was beginning to picture the charming girl from Hollywood, who appealed to men.

"After a bit more time—I don't recall exactly—she dropped me. No tiff happened or anything, she just moved on. I knew she was around and I saw her across the dance floor in nightclubs a couple of times—she had lost weight and was even prettier. The war ended but it still took eight months for Jimmy to be discharged. When he got out he took me out to Chasen's to celebrate and there she was. With some real swell. She didn't notice us but we were in the next booth and I was waiting to catch her eye, when I heard her speak and my mouth just fell open—"

Wanita stared off to her left, her mouth agape.

"What?" I asked.

"Well, she was talking like me. It wasn't just my pronunciation either, it was my voice itself. And, I mean, I knew my voice was what men liked. I'd seen men's glances go right by me until they heard me talk and then they were on me like bees on a honeysuckle. And when she did it, I could see why. I asked Jimmy to listen and he heard it too—he said, 'She sounds just like you. Who is she?' And even he was drawn in, 'cause I mean, you put my voice into a person who looked like Norma Jean and it was devastating. You bet I got him out of there fast."

She must have felt that I was sitting up straighter in my seat and peering over, trying to see if she was making all this up. "Don't look at me like that," she said. "I know I don't sound that way anymore. Isn't that just what I'm telling you about?

"I called Norma Jean up and asked to meet her and I could tell she knew what it was about. She came to see me, looking much more swank than before, wearing a white suit with light blue satin trim. She greeted me with a kiss, she exclaimed at how well I looked, she fussed over my bracelets and teased me about Jimmy—said she'd seen us leave—but I wasn't pleased because she did it all in *my* voice. Her own, you know, was a little shrill, and she sometimes stuttered.

"She saw it wouldn't wash. She sat down.

"'Don't be mad at me,' she said.

"'Talk like yourself,' I said.

"'I can't anymore, honey,' she said. 'I didn't just learn your way of speaking. I had to—I had to give mine up.'

"I goggled at that. 'What do you mean?'

"She said, 'You know, Wanita, the first time I heard your voice I felt that really it *was* mine. The way I was supposed to be, I mean. So I listened, I practiced, and then one day it was just the only way for me to speak. I can't even remember how I talked before.'

"'But honey,' I said, 'it isn't yours, it's mine.'

"'Wanita,' she said, 'I need it more than you do. You're going to marry that sweet Jimmy Blue Eyes and be happy talking just to him. You can leave Hollywood and go have that place you dreamed of.'

"'Actually, honey, we're going to be here for a while.' Did I mean to threaten her? I guess I did. 'Jimmy and I can both get work here and we'll have to save a long time before we can afford to buy land up north.'

"And Norma Jean said she could help us. And so, by God, I sold my voice to her."

✻

I said, "What?" I had been mesmerized, for as Wanita talked, I had been trying to catch the breathy speech of Marilyn Monroe somewhere behind her own deep tones.

"I sold her the right to my voice, the voice of Wanita Gregg, for a chunk of hillside in Lake County and twenty-seven years with Jimmy Donofrio."

"And you had to stop speaking that way yourself?"

"No, that happened later. This land belonged to the same man who owned the other piece, a producer. Norma Jean didn't really have any money then, but she got him to give us a mortgage on it—I guess she used herself as the downpayment. We didn't ask. We got married and drove up here in a '36 Ford and lived in a tent till Jimmy built the first cottage. We were in love, we were delighted. My dad came to live with us and Jimmy built another cabin for him, so he was with us but we had our privacy. Things were just getting going up here with the wine business. We didn't have the capital for that, but we leased our land and Jimmy also took sales jobs from time to time and we eked along. Later we had two kids, a son and a daughter, and Jimmy enlarged the big cottage and built the other two to rent out, but that never did work out, really—we just used the space ourselves. Jimmy had more ideas than sense, if you know what I mean.

"I think the first inkling I got of my problem was in 1952, when I was in the hospital in Sonoma having my son. I heard two nurses outside the room, laughing at me. They thought I was imitating her. Marilyn Monroe.

"When the baby was three months old I left him with my dad one day and went in to the movies—over in St. Helena—and listened for myself. You know, I hadn't felt so bad when I talked to her face to face, but movies magnify everything. And maybe I'd already gotten some distance from who I'd been.

"The first thing that upset me was the elocution. When I heard Marilyn Monroe I realized that when I was trying to sound so smart I just sounded dumber—she had gotten it exactly, you see, so you heard the correct pronunciation but also that shade of tentativeness of someone who had to work so very hard not to make a mistake and a kind of proud glee that she was pulling it off. So it was comical. Well, I dropped that instantly. I went back to my Okie from Lodi voice just fine—in fact, I probably already had, with my dad around. But that still didn't do it. I remember we went to a party—the launching of a winery in Napa, a friend of Jimmy's threw it—and *Gentlemen Prefer Blondes* was out and when I spoke, there were giggles. I pretended I had a cold, then, made myself hoarse. And after that—I tried to talk firmer and lower, but on many occasions, with strangers, I shut up altogether. And all this time she was getting more and more famous and inescapable."

Wanita leaned back in her chair and looked up at the stars, which were thick over the dark hillsides. "My dad, I'll say this for him, he never fell for her. As long as he lived—he died in 1956—he called her a poor imitation of me."

"And Jimmy?"

"Well, he said the same, but I didn't believe him. I got to thinking when he held me in the dark he imagined he was holding Marilyn Monroe. That shut me up too. And I was changing. Two kids, you know, you have to control them—I'd find myself yelling out across the hills, trying to get them home for dinner. You don't stay the same . . .

"But I kept sneaking out to see her movies, too, and each time, I'd learn something about myself. She sounded—I'd sounded— like somebody who'd just had sex. Not somebody all keyed up for sex—I always felt Ava Gardner had that sound, Lauren Bacall— deep and teasing. Marilyn Monroe sounded like someone who just had sex and was grateful, flattered even. It made men feel bolder because she—I—sounded like we'd already done it and we'd be sure to do it again. I noticed how they were casting opposite her. She didn't get the handsome young guys—it was all older men or wimps or someone totally naive like the cowboy in *Bus Stop*—and I decided it was because of her voice, because it had the effect of encouraging *unconfident* men. The bolder sorts like to go up against more of a challenge. So I realized something about Jimmy."

"That he wasn't confident?"

"You know, I grew up thinking men were a big deal," Wanita said, with a sigh. "I don't know where I got that idea—books, movies. It was literally years before I realized that Jimmy couldn't really do much of anything for long—that he'd been just a struggling saleman when the war came along. Which was no disgrace, but after a while it did start to get me that he was content to live for the rest of his life mostly off this land that came from a woman."

"Well, but he was paying it off."

"Oh no. Did I leave that out? She'd sent us money more than once—we really needed it then, too. Checks made out to the Wanita Gregg Donofrio Elocution School. Her joke. And then she paid off the whole mortgage, in the mid-fifties. It was a year before my dad died, 'cause I remember we told him. You see, I wanted to turn it down. Stupid, really. I thought that would somehow give me the right to my voice back—the right to be unselfconscious again. Well, anyway. There was no going back. But I noticed that neither my dad nor Jimmy had any problem taking the money my voice had earned us and I guess that bothered me. Certainly it was after that Jimmy started telling me I'd become grumpy and a nag about money. And I was always harping at the kids to study and work to make something of themselves. They have, too. Jim studied winemaking, even went over to France, and now he's working for a winery in Australia. Wendy's an oceanographer, knows everything about seaweed—you remind me of her, a little. Listen, let's open another bottle and drink to Marilyn Monroe."

She went inside and I noticed that I was feeling pretty crocked already, but somehow I didn't want to move and miss the end of the story. When Wanita came back out she had a merlot. "I actually bought this one," she said as she poured. She smelled it deeply before she drank. She seemed to have forgotten the toast.

I asked what happened after that.

"You know as much as me. After the mortgage was paid off, we didn't hear from her. I guess she felt she'd discharged the debt. But of course we heard about her. Successes. Divorces. Seems to me I was aware she had health problems—she lost her pregnancies, was into hospitals for rest. But it was only later all this other stuff came out."

I breathed the pungent breeze from her garden and thought of all the sad stories I'd heard about Marilyn Monroe.

"You ever see her when she sang Happy Birthday to JFK? If you believe even half of it her life was a mess. She should have been screeching, angry, scared, but there she was singing like the happiest piece of fluff on earth, like she was just taking a little break between fucks, pardon my language. See—her problem was she couldn't knock it off. No matter what, she sounded like grateful, dim, sexed-up Wanita Gregg, age twenty. Poor kid."

I was going to ask which kid she meant, young Wanita or MM, but as I went to speak I yawned and realized I was way drunk. I felt dizzy, like I was going to roll right down the hill and tumble in the creek.

"Cut both ways," she said. "On the one hand, she couldn't get anybody to take her seriously. She went East to study acting and it was like this big delicious joke—Marilyn studies Stanislavsky. People laughed when she even *said* Stanislavsky. On the other hand, she used to make those studio jackals kiss her ass if they wanted her to work, and it was always poor sweet child. Still is."

"So you resented her?"

"Sure I did. Now I don't. Or maybe I do. You always kind of want to have your silly young self back, don't you? I think because of her I toughened up too soon. I mean, you do as you age, anyway, but I . . . Sometimes I wonder whether, if I'd kept my voice, I'd have done something foolish, had affairs, run off. As it was, I kind of went into myself more. Especially after Jimmy got cancer—from cigarettes—he died too young, only fifty-six. And the kids went off, into the world, and I looked around and realized I'd become a recluse. Happens easily up here. It's beautiful and you forget you're alone."

I had slid off my chair and was sitting beside a bed of lavender, letting it tickle my face. I remember Wanita saying, musingly, "I always wished I had beautiful feet."

I think I laughed and hiccupped then and Wanita helped me up and put me to bed in the book cottage and I slept it off.

ℐ

In the morning, while she gave me some toast and juice, I asked her if all that story was true and she just cackled. "I jabbered more last night than I have in years. Don't know what I said."

And I told myself it couldn't be true. I took a shower out among the roses—something I'd been wanting to do—and standing naked and wet with their pure pink faces around me, I had a clear sense of what to tell Jill about her land.

I called her from my B & B (where they carefully didn't ask me why I'd been away all night). I stressed how inaccessible the land was, how much money and time would have to be put in just to get the road fixed, let alone electricity and water, then suggested she could leave it as it was and call it a wildflower preserve. I described some of the varieties I'd found there, including rare gentians that shouldn't be picked.

"That's it," said Jill, and she called me a genius some more as she told me she'd been approached about lending her name to a cosmetics line.

So I went home and waited while she got the deal lined up. I made a trip up in the fall to cultivate and seed some of the barer spots (flax, penstemons, blue-eyed grass—Jill wanted blues—but I put in Pink Maids And Kisses and Venus' Looking Glass, just for the names). And the following April there we were, back up in Geyserville, shooting some ads with Jill knee-deep in purple lupine, Jill in a white dress under the lilacs, Jill in old jeans, artlessly natural out in a fresh blue field. The art director loved the ruined house, romantic and worn. I borrowed some hanging fuchsias and rustic chairs for the porch from Wanita, who stayed inside as the crews from interview shows passed on their way to get Jill Santiago's eloquent defense of the healing powers of native plants.

The actual ingredients for the shampoo and skin cream, of course, came from elsewhere, and the factory was in Long Beach. Jill agreed with me that the property was unworkable for her; in fact, she had some choice things to say about the guy who sold it to her. When

I told her I'd someday like to retire to such a place myself, she consulted Coolidge (the accountant) and sold it to me at a (tax deductible) loss. I'm pretty sure she was such a doll because she liked my work. Though it's true I dropped the fact that I knew, from her ex-boyfriend Paul (yes, he blabbed), that she got the surreal extravagance of her curves by taking out her bottom pair of ribs.

※

I go up when I can to work on the house (I'm letting the meadow evolve). Wanita treats me with amused tolerance, though since we've become neighbors it's awkward to confide. I keep remembering the afternoon we were having a good-bye drink, after Jill had finished and gone home. We sat outside, in the garden, watching the men from the winery work, and I asked her again if that story had been true.

She took a swig of cabernet, gargled with it, and swallowed, dimpling a bit and touching her piled white hair. Then she looked over at the viner who was driving in some stakes and said, "Honey, you oughtn't to work so hard in the hot sun. You could get—" a little breath— "sunstroke."

"Hey, pretty good," he said. "Marilyn Monroe, right?"

She looked at me, triumphant. I was stunned. Her voice had been a powder puff, a cobweb of sex. "Do it again," I said.

She shook her head. "I should keep my big mouth shut. Go on back to the land of the cannibals," she said. "But watch out."

"They won't get me," I said.

"No?" she asked. I can still hear the softness of her voice.

Meet the Impersonators!
(1986)

Accounts

This morning I go over to the house early, so Saran and I can do the accounts before practice. Spring just hit Pittsburgh and we have a sweet morning, sunny, snow gone, birds singing their asses off. I walk along, feeling sort of good and sort of terrible, still delicately drunk.

When I get there, Billy White is sitting on a couch in the front yard with his hands over his face. The couch is the one Amy made from the seat of an old car. Uncomfortable, but free.

I say his name, touch his shoulder.

He looks up. "Sue Drum," he says.

"Good morning."

"Oh, Sue Drum," he says, and starts crying again.

Well, it looks right, so I sit down beside him and start crying too. It's easy; all I have to do is think of Nash just out of the shower and waggling his body around. I cry a while and then the crying intensifies my headache and I'm starting to remember last night and I have Billy all over me, his wet face against my shirt, so I stop and try to find out what his problem is.

Billy's a twenty year old from the suburbs, a cute blond kid. He wears black all the time, black pegged pants, expensive black jacket, black Beatle boots with Paul's signature on the heel. He tries to be a tight tough guy with a bitter grin, but what he is is nice. Saran was pretty in love with him for a while, but she has a rule against that. So his story is no surprise. After a lot of sniffling and choked pauses, it comes out to this:

After the party died, Billy slept in the living room. This morning around nine Amy recruited him to help her and her boyfriend move this couch out of her place on the third floor because she's found a better one. So Billy and the boyfriend started lugging this mother down but got stuck at the second floor bend. They shoved too hard against the wall—it's just fiberboard—that closes off Saran's room and the wall fell in and there they were staring at Saran in bed with the bass player from The Coup.

"Well, he's a shitty bass player," I say. Billy clouds up again so I study the wooden scrollery on the house across the street and wonder whether my stomach will accept food.

"I know how she is," he says. "She needs a lot of guys, she's insecure. It's just seeing her there . . . her naked . . . she *screamed* at me . . ."

"Well, Billy, have you considered? I mean, would it help you if you were sleeping with someone else yourself?"

"No way," he says. "She'd never trust me again. Besides, it's one of her rules. She'd drop me in a flash. You know Saran."

I do. I get up and go inside. Living room's trashed—empty keg in a tub of water, pizza boxes, that horrible stale smell of Party. In the kitchen I blow my nose on a paper towel and put a pot of water on. The stove is gummy with God knows what. I find the jar of instant okay, but I look all over and can't find a single spoon, clean or dirty. I take a mug out of the dishrack and scrub it, thinking about Billy's story. I don't like it. Means more trouble between Saran and Amy. Dissension and self-doubt are the destroyers of bands. I drink a mug of water, make coffee—shake too much out of the jar but it would have tasted lousy anyway—and carry it upstairs.

It's funny how you get used to a name. When I met Saran Velcro she was with the Products, hard core band. She tuned her guitar so she could put her fingers straight across the frets and have a major chord. Looked terrible, weird, her hand a white bar across the neck. She turned her head from the mike to play so her voice got lost. It drove me nuts, for her voice was like aluminum, strong, silvery, with a crinkle to it. She knew she had a voice and the Products had no songs. So we started up a girl group—the Tramps, the Cramps, Green Venus—we were fumbling then, before we became the Impersonators. She kept Saran Velcro; it's her; you forget what it means to other people. Of course, I've been Sue Drum since I was seventeen, but my name was Drummond. Nobody knows what Saran was.

Her room is at the front of the narrow woodframe house. The wall is propped back up so I knock on the door.

She lets me in. "Hi there, Lollipop," she says. She flops onto the mattress and I kneel cautiously, the coffee shaky in my hands. That's what there is, a mattress and a TV and Saran's four outfits pinned with hatpins to the walls. "Did you hear what Amy pulled on me this morning?" she asks. "There I am in bed with Ray—you know, the bass player from The Coup?—fucking away and suddenly the *wall* falls in. Can you believe it? Nine in the morning the little decorator decides to move the furniture. And don't tell me she didn't know we were in here. Why else did she get Billy? Can you believe it? The wall, the fucking wall, falls—right—*in*."

"Ummhmm, Billy's out front. He told me."

"Billy's outside?" She lifts the shade and opens the window, leans out. "Hey there, Peanuts," she yells, "why don't you go out and get us some breakfast?" I hear Billy ask what she wants. "Oh, orange juice, doughnuts, champagne, you *know*, breakfast. Thank you, baby." She tumbles back in, opens the other window too, and spring fills the room. The light catches the blue tint in her short dark hair. In her sweater and panties she looks about eighteen, though I know she's older than me and I'm twenty-five. "Did you see Ray last night?" she asks. "Isn't he killer cute?"

"I don't know, Saran. He's a shitty bass player. He lags."

"He lags," she agrees sadly. "And what happened to you last night?"

I sip my coffee. "I went to bed."

"Yes?" she says. "Who with?"

"Come on, Saran, let's get the accounts done."

"You know you can't wait your whole life for Lawrence Nash to come back. It's been months. He left, he's gone, come on. The only way to get over a guy is to replace him. That's what all the people in the *National Enquirer* do."

I just look at her. What can I say?

"O-kay." She sobers. "Business. We have to do the accounts, practice, then somebody has to get the van from the shop and—you talked to that sound man last night and arranged things, right? So then we'll go over to the club and set up and have us a home-coming gig. The Impersonators home from their triumphal tour—let's see if we made any money."

She goes to the office to get the account book and while she's gone I make the bed—that is, I smooth out the sheets and use the blanket for a spread, so we won't lose all our little scraps of paper. Saran has told me that when she left her husband she resolved to live unencumbered. No more than one room. No more than four outfits. There's no one else living on the second floor since I moved, but Saran keeps to this cubicle and if she buys a new top an old one must go. Usually she sticks me with them.

She comes back and we settle down to work. After a while, Billy brings in orange juice, scrambled eggs, bacon, whole wheat toast; he really takes care of Saran. I eat some toast.

My part of doing the accounts consists of staring at receipts and remembering what they're for. Saran's got it worked out so everything is tax deductible if we can just record it all. The fact is, she's got the arrangements so complicated I never can quite follow them. The house is rented by Instant Babes Productions (IBP), which is us, incorporated, as managers. IBP owns the office. Then the band rents the basement from IBP, to use for practice. Amy rents the third floor and Saran this room and they split the kitchen. I'm not sure who owns the living room, or my room since I moved. We each have shares in the band—I get extra because I write the music. And we each have shares in the management—Saran gets extra for doing the booking. Amy gets extra for doing the costumes and posters. But really everything goes for expenses like the van and recording. Our first on vinyl—an Extended Play—has paid itself back now and we're saving for a full album.

This trip was the best we've had. The E.P. title song, "Love is the Great Crippler of Young Adults," is our hit, and wherever the college radio stations are playing it we had crowds. Of course, there was Dayton, where we got four people shooting pool and they left, and in Richmond the club had gone out of business when we got there, but at least we broke even and then we sold a lot of records and cassettes. Saran has piles of cash out on the bed and is making out deposit slips: "Album account, household . . ."

"What about equipment?"

"I thought we'd better get the van fixed first. You want more electronic toys? We'll see how much we make tonight."

I move closer to the window to let the sun hit my cheek. "What kind of deal did you get?"

"The door, but he said he'd guarantee a hundred. The cover's two-fifty. Now, here's the forty bucks the band owes you."

I take the money. "Saran, I've been thinking I should take a job. My place is cheap but I'm not quite making it."

She leans back against the pillow, shrewd now and grown up. "You can move back in here."

She knows I don't want to. I moved out to live with Nash and I want to stay right where he left me. I say, "I think things are more peaceful this way."

"Peaceful for who?" she says, but I don't bite. "Well, okay, Petunia, get a job. What'll you do, waitress?"

"Mmm, I hate waitressing, but I don't know if I can get anything else. With my hair shaved up around my ear like this, you know, people think it's freaky."

"Who thinks it's freaky?" she says. "Men who scrape the whiskers off their faces? Women with waxed legs?"

"Oh, come on, Saran, I did it to be freaky."

"Well, simple," she says. "Just get a wig. Go in disguise as normal."

"That'd make a good song title," I say. "In Disguise As Normal."

"Here's a check, all made out—you fill in the amount when you get the van and make sure you get a receipt. They inspected it and put on two new tires."

"God, it passed inspection?"

"Yup," she says. "They just puttied in some of the holes. You have to pick it up by five. I'm going to run out to the bank now and make these deposits and then I'll be back and if Amy shows up we can practice." Saran stands on the bed and takes down her pink shirt, lace vest, and velvet mini.

"Where did Amy go?"

Saran pulls off her sweater, smells it, says, "This is shot. Amy? She went off to pick up her new couch. That druggie banker boyfriend of hers bought it. She told me not to nail the wall back up because this one's even bigger. God *damn* that little bitch." Saran steps into her skirt and almost falls on the account book.

"I'm sorry you were embarrassed."

"Who said anything about being embarrassed?" Saran cries, her voice sailing. "Do you know they bashed the wall in just as I was finally about to *come*?"

RHYTHM SECTION

Amy and I are watching TV. It's almost two and Saran isn't back from the bank. Amy doesn't want to practice anyway; she says we played so much on tour we'll just be stale tonight if we practice now.

Actually, she didn't say that. She said, "The tour wore us to perfection." When Amy's straight, she's almost incoherent. You have to know what she means to know what she means.

Sometimes I think of Amy as an optical illusion. You see her soft brown eyes, soft crewcut with the sweet little braid at the nape. Looking so clean in her round-collared blouses—I mean, *blouses*. She wears slips. She's been a drug runner, a dabbler at the edge of crime. She's dated hoods. She can get you anything. She seems to like exotic mixes: Cocaine and valium. Quaaludes and mushrooms. She talks then; if you met her you'd think she was fine—pretty, bright, a trifle heavy. She was brought up to look innocent in Ohio. I've met her parents, pale folk who speak blandness when they speak at all. It's like having trees for parents, she once said.

The name of the band came from Amy. She was taking a course at the university and read this feminist who said that all women were female impersonators. It struck her funny. "All people are human impersonators," she said, and we agreed.

I am feeling a bit better. Amy made me cream of chicken soup and tea. We carried her new couch up here to her place and reassembled Saran's wall. Amy's new couch is turquoise with silver threads, has pointy legs and arms like wings, an early 60's couch, a rocketship. Amy likes turquoise and pink, she's the one who sprayed all the appliances in the kitchen with metalflake car paint.

On TV a pregnant woman tells her divorced friend, "When you find the right man, you won't have any questions at all. And you won't be afraid of anything. Not anything."

Amy and I laugh. "Girl courage," Amy says.

I say, "Hmmhmm, you feel sooo certain. And then when they screw up you fight down doubt; doubt itself will prove you were mistaken."

"But, well, the thing is," Amy says, "he's Kid Orchid now."

"You know I hate that name. Kid Orchid, he's some pop tart on MTV. He's not Nash."

Amy sighs and offers me more tea.

She's a sweet person. I say, "Amy, you know what it's like when you're straight and everyone else is high? That's nothing to chastity. People look grotesque, wiggling towards each other, smiling like fools at things that aren't funny. So—last night I was talking to this sound man—you know how I love wiring and stuff and so—I went over to his place to see his sound board and we—you know. I wish I hadn't done it. God, I hate being back here. I didn't mind when we were on the road. On the road you wake up, you travel, do a sound check, do a show; I could always imagine Nash still back here. And till last night I could pretend he could come back any time and nothing would have changed. Now, what am I?"

"Sue Drum," she says.

"That's right, I'm Sue Drum." On TV, a woman is bragging about her control of her husband's cholesterol. "I think I'll go downstairs for a while and work on songs."

"I can get some opium," she says. "Or acid."

PERCUSSION

1. A half an hour on my drums and I am clear in a way I am nowhere else. I get into a place between thought and dream. Lately I find myself contemplating instruments. What is an instrument. And what is not.

2. Once upon a time—before Edison I guess—an instrument was a device you plucked, blew through, or hit to make a noise. The thing could amplify your effort and regulate it, divide it into notes, one note different from another. No music before the instrument?

3. Lord, I am but the instrument of Thy will. I seem to remember that. If man is God's instrument, could God make any music before man?

4. Thomas Alva Edison invented the phonograph. I like to think he restored music to the state it was in before transcription. I don't like written music. But then, I can't read it. Once it's recorded you can listen to it and imitate, just like in Africa among the master drummers. But then, why imitate when you can spin the platter again? And so we began to live with the ghosts of musicians.

5. There was some big fuss when Dylan went electric. Betraying the natural, the acoustic folk. As if the bell of the horn, the

shell of the drum, weren't doing all they could to make our noises bigger. As if guitars grew in the woods.

But it is true that the electric instrument and its companions, amp, fuzz box, echo effect, made new sounds. And they could survive a greater violence. You could jump on the instrument, flail it around, break it, and music became its suffering outcry.

6. Now, we have given the instrument memory. It can sample and contain the ghost of many noises. My Mattel tom tom recalls my touch indefinitely. When Saran and I were in Washington pushing the E.P. at every alternative record store, we found one where they sold old instruments. I picked up an accordion, and Saran admitted she played one as a child. Though Saran won't concede anymore that she isn't a great guitarist, it seemed to me a possibility to switch her to keyboards. So I traded a few "Love is the Great Cripplers" for the accordion. Then in the van I found its lung had sprung a leak. Saran said she hated the accordion because it hid her—I guess it hid her little tits-to-be. Amy replaced the fabric and ribs with transparent plastic and I took out the keyboard and installed an old Casio I got cheap when they revised their models. Now I can program it with samba, cha-cha, the sound of clarinet and violin, and pumping the clear air in and out is pure empty activity. Now it is my Memory Squeezebox.

7. Nash believes in the digital, he says the compact disk will soon take over, and the computer. A drum machine is already cheaper than a drum kit, he says, and I will be replaced. I don't know. Hitting something to make a sound—kids do it in their cribs. Is it the exertion of the body or the planning mind that makes the music? And what about the invention that comes out of you, surprising you, in the moment of playing?

When Nash went, he left behind his old records. He said he would get it all on c.d. and have it perfect forever. But me, I love their scratches and pops, their history of being played. Like us, they can't remember without cost, without acquiring layers of beautiful damage.

8. I taught myself to play when I was sixteen and my dad was dying. I could do what I wanted as long as I stayed out of everyone's way, even though before that I'd been told a hundred times that drums weren't appropriate for a girl. Dying, Dad watched TV and let the others talk around him as if nothing bad was happening. Half of the garage had been his workshop. I set up my kit there and played along with records on the small stereo I plugged in on his workbench. Sometimes, to please him, I'd use his old albums—big band stuff, Sinatra and Dean Martin, and when I did, he'd tell me I was getting pretty good, so I knew he could hear me. More than anything, I wanted to be loud.

9. You can tell everything about musicians by the instruments they pick. Wind instruments, sax, harmonica—those guys are all face, all head. Keyboardists favor throb and dexterity, wail, groan, plea. Sentimentalists, sufferers. Guitarists? I used to watch Nash fingering fingering fingering and get crazy, guitar is both phallus and hole, guitar is sex, self-sufficient.

Drums? Everybody knows drums are structured anger.

10. I like a silence. Nash and I studied those 60's songs that still had silence in them. They used a choked guitar, Farfisa, and a voice. Now with all these tracks you can record on, the temptation is to fill them. To be a musician you have to have restraint. Music marries silence.

11. And when my mouth upon him made him whimper, was he then my instrument?

12. I am always sad when, as now, I take my kit apart to move it. I think of the drums stacked up to go as corpses. Nothing as sad as the instrument abandoned.

TORCH

The van is up on the lift. I look at the underside, rusting and ungainly, the low belly of the gas tank, the rectal exhaust. The mechanic moves around it tightening the nuts with the hydraulic and then puts each hubcap on with two clean blows of his fist. And circles again, twice, touching the tires, hardly looking. He isn't going to let me rush him. Then it comes down with a sigh, the Impersonators' van, painted in Amy's colors, patches of putty showing gray where it had rusted through. When I give the mechanic the check, he hardly looks at me. To these guys all women fuss and I'm just another fussy woman.

I drive over to the house. We have definitely blown off practice. Billy White says he will come and pick me up, so I walk home to get ready. It's cloudy but still warm. The fancy grocery has moved some of its produce outside and I pause. California strawberries. I have forty bucks. A crazy man starts asking me if strawberries are good, are they good, are they?

It makes me go into the bar next door to buy a sixpack. The young man behind the bar has a little fold of extra skin on his upper lip, a permanent pucker. He'd be surprised how kissable I find it.

Walking along, the beer cold in the crook of my arm, I try to think of someplace else to go. When I get to my building I sit on the front steps. The wind rises, with rain in it.

I start my first beer on my way up the stairs.

Since I got back, I've been taking down the Nash collage that fills our apartment. The first part was easy because it was all Kid Orchid stuff: posters, reviews, radio station playlists, interviews, even the concert ticket he sent me for New York. Now what's left up is Nash. Kid Orchid is a pile of paper on the floor, in every picture wearing more and more makeup, fewer and fewer clothes. "Pop tart." Nash taught me that term. The first thing I fell in love with was his phrasing. When I met him, I was asking for a refund on a dead patch cord at Radio Shack, insisting that I didn't break it. Nash stood nearby listening and followed me out to say, "That took a lot of tit." I said, "Tit?" looking down at myself. "That's like nerve, balls. In a woman," he said, "it's tit." In interviews Kid Orchid says junk like, "The second album will be my most definitive." You see? He can't be Nash. How can a man remove his sense of humor?

When I met him, Lawrence Nash just wanted to make a living with his music. Have a studio in his basement. What we all want. He put down three beers one two three and told me he had licked his drinking problem. He was sleeping at a friend's place, working part time at Hardee's, teaching about twenty kids guitar. He wore old shirts and jackets from the Goodwill, huge shouldered things, because he thought he was too skinny. After he left, I would watch Perry Mason reruns and be comforted by Perry's breadth, his shoulders filling my TV. His dark, circled eyes promised me justice.

Now here's a sign from the very start of Orchid. I remember it was his first gig after the Rods & Cones kicked him out. He made up his face like Jean Shrimpton, a sweet 60's face with eyelashes painted on and soft freckles and a pale pout. One dangling earring to show he was "pierced as women are," as his song goes. He scissored one sleeve and shoulder out of his suit and wore a tie. After he copied the photograph, he lettered around it quotes from invented critics: "Fabulously febrile and hectic." "Utterly gaspworthy." "New York psychopop." And people showed up—lots of kids. How soon after that was it when he said to me, "I want a Rolls Royce that runs so quiet, it might be fueled with pearls." Here's his album: *Disorient Express.* "Hypnotically inconclusive," reviews said. "Dada Americana." It's full of all the trash he likes: wispy psychedelia, the corniest of country western, Connie Francis, glitterrock. I can even hear an imitation of his father, an old schmooze crooner, singing "Moonlight Bay"—*you have stolen my heart plunkaplunkaplunkaplunk now don't go way . . .*

Last night when I came home I tore down all the quotes we'd put up around our bed. Well, I was drunk. When I woke up the bed was full of staples sticking me. And quotes. Here's a lyric by the Piss Clams that rhymes "dancer," "cancer," and "romance her." Nash thought that was "bril"—"bril" for brilliant, I think he got that from an English magazine. Here's one I chose, Ray Charles: "We don't want to be famous, we just want to be great."

I take my second beer into the shower. Nothing feels as wonderful as drinking cold beer from the bottle while hot water pounds your neck. Well. There are other things that feel better but I don't have them anymore. I shampoo, shave my legs, my underarms. When I get out I wipe off the mirror and towel my wet hair over to one side. There's blond bristle now—it's been about a week. I use shaving cream because my scalp is sensitive. I shave a careful curve around my ear. I comb my hair back, brush my bangs forward. Even now I think it's pretty because Nash liked it. I was the woman who Nash wanted. It freaked me out to have him disappear. I used to think I could get him into bed and love him back into Nashness. Sometimes it worked. He'd roll off, the two of us would lie there warm in a second skin of sweat, and he'd tell me dreams. He'd be scared then of Kid Orchid's success. I took these moods to be the truest truth.

Tonight I'll wear my low-in-the-front green metallic dress, the one Nash called my mermaid outfit, black tights, my silver sneakers. I put in my techno-earrings, green and silver, made out of tiny fuses. Better not drink another beer unless I eat. I get a bowl of cereal—there isn't any milk so I use orange juice—and take it out onto our little glassed-in porch. With the stereo on I stretch out on the couch. Ella Fitzgerald. It must have rained while I was in the shower. When I open the casement windows the wind comes in fresh, sweet with water. Bird cries chop Ella's song. Far off, I hear the looping siren of an ambulance. The light that makes it through the ivy vines catches the edges of my furniture. The white table, the yellow pitcher, the blue jar, seem composed by some woman whose life must be strict and lovely.

Ella is pretty old on this record. But still it's wonderful torch; her voice on the lowest notes has the quality of pure love, love maintained when the guy is gone, no anger, no hope, just the pour of feeling for its own sake, nothing, not even pride, to be achieved by it.

Last night when I came in I called Nash. On the answering

machine his voice jabbered. It made me think of the time he did so much speed he shivered all day and I could see his heartbeat push his chest. It made me want to hold him till he quieted. Somewhere in New York my voice on tape is waiting to say, "Baby, I don't know my name and number."

Homecoming Gig

Ride in My Little Chevette

There's always something promiscuous about a singer. Saran goes from emotion to emotion, song to song. Excited over him and him and him. Her attention flickering to where it meets attention.

Nash, you bastard, where are you tonight?

Van Gogh A Go Go

What a terrible song. How could I have written anything this crude and stupid? Each time we put it on the playlist, I think it'll be okay and then when I'm in the midst of it I realize it's horrible. I should never have wound up writing songs. When I listened to my radio as a kid, I would follow bassline, rhythm. Words broke down into the voice's gasp, fragmented by the beat. Now here I am, pounding my own words to pieces.

Testosterone

Love is when you know everything that's wrong with him, his failing to clean the bathroom and then calling you pig for a dirty hairbrush, his egotism, his black fury, his unfair unfair unfair sexuality and still you let him get inside you. That's a woman's love. That's love. It's the sickest thing going.

End of the first set. Before I can get away, here's the sound man coming up. "Sounds good," he says.

I crouch down and adjust the old pillow inside my bass. "I can't hear too well—we need more monitor. Have you got Saran's guitar too high? This isn't thrash metal, you know. I want more of a chiming sound."

"Okay," he says. "Is something wrong?" Eye contact.

"Mm-mm. Where's the wasamba? You see a thing that looks like a rattle?" I sort of crawl away from him around my kit. Over by the bar I see Saran and Amy talking. I know they're discussing me. I glare at them but they don't notice. That damn Saran has Billy in the corner, Ray from The Coup up front.

I fiddle with the high hat. The sound man, seen from down here, is a well-built guy wearing a sharkskin jacket, jeans, nice modern gray shoes.

"Are you upset about last night?" he says. "You left so fast." He crouches down beside me.

"I was drunk last night."

"You were? You didn't seem drunk." Eye contact.

"We'd been drinking since two in the afternoon. I was very drunk."

"But you're not drunk now."

"Not that drunk."

"So are you trying to say it was all," eye contact, "liquor. Because it seemed to me—"

I say, "Look, I'm sorry, I'm not really interested. Take what you got, that's it."

"Women are easy to get," he stands, "and hard to keep. Everybody gets that backwards."

"Good line," I say, as Amy's coming up.

She says, "Sue Drum, band conference." I follow her down through the bar into the kitchen.

Saran, back here with a pitcher, pours me a glass of beer. I test the counter—much too dirty to sit on. Amy starts to fiddle with my dress, which gets bunched up in the back when I play. I brush her away. "About time you came to my rescue."

"I thought you wanted to talk to him, Goldfish," Saran says.

"No way."

"That's what Amy said. What did he do to you last night?"

"Oh, nothing. We just sort of rolled around and it was terrible." I drain my beer, pour myself another.

Saran says, "Sex is always better when it starts worse and you work up to it. Those fast heavy fucking things just leave you happy-sore with nothing more to say."

"You should know," I mumble.

"What?"

"Great crowd tonight," Amy says. She's started turning around in place. She has one eye elaborately made up, the other plain.

"Yeah," says Saran, "and only about fifteen of them on the guest list. We're making money. What do you want, Sue Drum? We'll buy you something."

I finish my beer.

"Maybe we should get you a ticket to New York," Saran says.

"Fuck you too," I say.

"Helping others is so irritating," Amy says. "It's no wonder only saints can do it." She's cute, spinning around, her eyes hallucinatory in the fluorescent light.

I see that I've got both of them against me, which means at least I've patched up this morning's rift. And we're playing well tonight, and it's my band, so I go over and apologize and Amy hugs me and Saran closes in and huddles too.

For the rest of the break I sit outside with Billy White, holding hands.

Penalty for Early Withdrawal

The club has filled up. The sound man has given us more monitor and I can hear; we are making some *noise* now. We drop it down in the middle so Saran can say, "Hello everybody. We're the Impersonators, glad to be back home. Everybody get off your ass and *move*."

When the dancing starts, the other musicians are always points of stillness. There's Saran's Ray in his seat, smoking.

Over all the heads, I can see the sound man, serious behind his board and speakers. His name, I remember, is Mike. I made a joke last night that we were like people in some medieval guild, named by our profession. He meets my eyes, nods, and charges up the levels some more.

Shoot Me I'm Famous

Last night the sound man bent me back across his bed, his wolf mouth bigger than mine, so I could feel my head inside his jaws. I was lofty, drunk. He kept threatening me with satisfactions.

What surprises me is the tenacity of love, its deep drag. I can't get rid of the delusion that it matters. What will happen to Lawrence Nash now that he isn't the man I'm faithful to? Now that he's only the guy before last?

Pretty Girls Don't Spit

When finally for certain Nash was leaving town, I didn't ask to go along. I knew he didn't want me. I wouldn't beg. Wouldn't give him the pleasure. Maybe I didn't really want to go.

I'd cried all weekend, lost five pounds, my voice was rasping. Nash cooked me a special dinner the night before and burned the steak, and in the morning I could still smell smoke. Nash was extra considerate, left me the stereo even though it was mostly his, wrote down his new unlisted number and stapled it above the bed. I lay there; I hadn't moved since the middle of the night when we made love for the last time, the last time, the last time, that thought my rhythm while he was careful and sweet and excited—what excited him?—the last time, the last time.

He was all packed and waiting for his cab. He sat beside me on the bed. "Are you okay?" he said. "You look beat."

"Thanks a lot."

"You look pretty but tired," he said. "You know you always look good. Your new boyfriend will tell you so, too."

"No."

"Yes, baby," he said. "You'll be okay. You've still got a good fifteen years of heartbreaking left." He held me and I wrapped myself around him, arms and legs. I took his finger into my mouth. "I'm sorry, baby," he whispered, "I just don't want to be in love with anyone right now."

I hugged him tighter. "You'll be back," I said, "after Kid Orchid dies."

He laughed. "Sue Drum, you've got such a lot of tit."

Last time I touched him his hair was damp, his earring scratched my cheek.

Love is the Great Crippler of Young Adults

> *Right now, someone you know*
> *is falling*
> *one of millions destined to be*
> *confined to homes*
> *Won't, won't you help?*
> *Can you stand by and see it spread unchecked?*
> *Passed from mouth to mouth in cars,*
> *in movie houses,*
> *within our very schools?*
> *Love is the great crippler*
> *Love is the great crippler*
> *Love is the great crippler of young adults—*

The crowd is singing, I can see their mouths move in unison.

> *Symptoms have been known for centuries:*
> *Fever. Loss of direction.*
> *Voices memorized and words ignored.*
> *Don't, don't be distracted*
> *by attractive early signs. Listen to victims later:*
> *Follow the bruised lady buying babyfood.*
> *Smell the drunk man crying on the curb.*
> *Watch your local newspaper for word of murder—*
> *Love is the great crippler . . .*

Saran is a shimmering howl. The kids dance, hurling themselves together, shoulder to shoulder.

One hundred percent incidence of relapse.
Can't a cure be found?
Please help us
stop, stop this tragic malady today.
Send your donation.
If you're within the sound of my voice
ignore my lips and listen to my words:
Give—generously—
The heart you save may be your own.
Love is the great crippler . . .

When I hit the drum, the people move. It's simple. Hit the drum. People move. Hit it. The floor of the club is shaking. And the walls.

ELVIS LIVES

"Vegas ahead—see that glow?" said Mr. Page. "That's the glow of money, babes."

Lee looked up. All the way from Phoenix he'd ignored the others in the car and watched the desert as it turned purple and disappeared, left them rolling through big nothingness. Now lights filled his eyes as they drove into town. Lights zipped and jiggled in the night. Ain't it just like humans, he thought, to set up all this neon, like waving fire in the dark to scare away the beasts, to get rid of your own fear. Lights ascended, filling in a tremendous pink flamingo. There was something silly about Las Vegas—he laughed out loud. "What's so funny, man?" the kid, Jango, asked with that flicker in the upper lip he'd been hired for, that perfect snarl.

Lee shrugged and leaned his cheek against the car window, studying the lights.

"He's just happy 'cause we're finally here," said Baxter. "Here where the big bucks grow and we can pick some, right?" Baxter was a good sort, always carrying Lee and the kid. A pro.

"Just you remember, babes, we're here to collect the bucks, not throw 'em down the slots." Mr. Page pulled into the parking lot of the Golden Pyramid Hotel and Casino. On a huge marquee, yellow on purple spelled out E L V I S, then the letters danced around till they said L I V E S. The lights switched to a display of Elvis's face. "They do that with a computer," said Mr. Page.

Lee, Baxter, and Jango were silent, staring up. The same look came over them, a look that spoke of steamy dreams and sadness women wanted to console. The face—they all three had it. Three Elvises.

※

It was surely a strange way to make a living, imitating another man. Sometimes Lee thought he was the only one of them who felt its full weirdness. As they moved their gear into the suite the hotel provided for Talent, the others seemed to take it all for granted. Of course, Baxter had been doing Elvis for ten years. And the kid thought this was just a temporary gig that would bankroll a new band, a new album, where he'd be his punk-rock self, Jango. But Lee had never been in show business before. Maybe that was why it kept striking him as something horrifying, bringing the dead to life.

He threw his suitcase on a bed and went out to the living room where the bar was stocked for Talent. He poured himself a whiskey and carried it back to sip while he unpacked. Or maybe, Lee thought, he was just getting into the role, like Mr. Page said to, understanding Elvis Presley's own hollow feeling. He played the sad, sick Elvis, after all. Maybe his horror was something the man had had himself in his later years as he echoed his own fame.

Lee snapped open his old leather suitcase, the same valise his mamma had forty years ago when she was on her honeymoon and getting pregnant with him. "Why buy something new?" he'd said when Cherry pestered him before their trip to New York that started all the trouble. "This is leather, the real thing—you can't get that anymore."

Cherry admired fresh vinyl, though. Her wish for new things was so strong it tore her up, he could see. Game shows made her cry. She entered sweepstakes, stayed up late at night thinking of new ways to say why she should win in twenty-five words or less. There was so little he could give her, he *had* to let her enter him in the contest the Bragg *Vindicator* ran. New York wanted, as part of its Statue of Liberty extravaganza, dozens of Elvis Presley imitators, and Bragg, Tennessee, was going to send one. Cherry had always fancied he resembled Elvis—she used to roll around with delight when he'd sing "hunka hunka burnin' love" to her in bed. She borrowed a cassette deck and sent a tape of him in, along with a Polaroid taken once at a Halloween party.

When he won, Lee said he didn't have the voice for it, that great voice, but they said no one would notice, there'd be so many others up there, he could mouth the words. He could too sing, Cherry said—oh, she still loved him then—he sang just beautifully in church. There was little enough Cherry was proud of him for anymore. They still lived in the trailer on his mamma's land, and now that he'd put it on a cement foundation and built on a porch it seemed all the more permanently true that they were never going to have it any better. He was picking up what jobs he could as an electrician since the profit went out of farming and their part of the country got depressed. A free trip to the Big Apple was maybe what they needed.

And it was fun. Lee liked the pure-dee craziness of the celebration, a whole city in love with itself. Cherry bought one of those Lady Liberty crowns and wore it with a sexy white dress she'd made with just one shoulder to it. When they were riding on the ferry he heard a man say, looking at them, "Duplication is America's fondest dream," and the man's friend laughed and answered, "Such is identity in a manufacturing nation." Lee glared at them, *I ain't a duplicate*, and anyway, he noticed, they both had the same fifties' sunglasses and wrinkled jackets as everyone in soda-pop commercials. But when he got to rehearsal with all the other Elvises, he knew that, yes, it was hard to see them as real men instead of poor copies.

Because he had some age and gut on him, they put him toward the back, which was just fine. He didn't even feel too embarrassed during the show. After, he and Cherry were partying away when a white-haired man, very sharp in his Western-tailored suit, came up and said Lee was just what was needed. Lee laughed loudly and said, "Oh, go on," but Cherry put Mr. Page's card inside her one-strap bra.

And when they were back home and Cherry sighing worse than ever over the slimy thin blond people on *Knots Landing*, Mr. Page showed up, standing on their porch with a big smile. Cherry had called him, but Lee couldn't be mad—it meant she thought he was good for something.

Mr. Page's plan was a show like a biography of Elvis in songs. And he wanted three impersonators. For the kid Elvis, who drove a truck and struggled and did those first Sun sessions and Ed Sullivan, he'd found Jango, a California boy with the right hips and snarl. He had Baxter, who had experience doing Elvis at his peak, the movie star, the sixties Elvis. And he wanted Lee to be late Elvis, Elvis in gargantuan glittery costumes, Elvis on the road, Elvis taking drugs, Elvis strange, Elvis dying. "It's a great part, a tragic role," said Mr. Page. "The King—unable to trust anyone, losing Priscilla, trapped by his own fame—lonely, yes, tormented, yes, but always singing."

"Have you heard me sing?" Lee asked. He was leaning against the fridge in the trailer, drinking a beer.

Mr. Page beamed at his pose, at his belly. "Why, yes," he said. "I listened to the tape your lovely wife sent. You have a fine voice, big whatchacallit, baritone. So you break up a bit now and then or miss a note—that's great, babes, don't you see, it's his emotion, it's his ruin. You'll be beautiful."

And Cherry's eyes were shining and Mr. Page signed Lee up.

⁂

"Check, check, one two three," Baxter said into the mike. His dark Presley tones filled the Pharaoh's Lounge, where they'd spent the morning setting up.

"Man, what a system," Jango said to Lee. "If they'd let me do my stuff, my real stuff, on a system like this, I'd be starsville in a minute."

Lee looked over at the kid, who was leaning against an amp in the black leather suit he'd had made after they played Indianapolis. Jango wasn't saving a penny, really—he kept buying star gear.

"Yeah, one of these nights," Jango said, "when I'm in the middle of a number—'All Shook Up,' I think—I'm just gonna switch right into my own material. You remember that song I played you, 'Love's a Tumor'?"

Lee grinned and finished his can of beer. Worst song he'd ever heard in his life.

"Yeah, they'd be shook up then, all right," said Jango.

Mr. Page came over to them. "Go hit some high notes on there, kid," he said, "let's check out the treble." While Jango went over to the mike, Mr. Page said to Lee, "How you doing?"

Lee squatted down by the Styrofoam cooler they always stashed behind the drummer's platform, fished out a Coors, popped it open, stood drinking.

"You seem a little down, babes. Can I do something?"

"You can let me out of the contract so I can go on home," Lee said.

"Now, why should I do that? I could never find somebody else as good as you are. Why, you're the bleakest, saddest Elvis I've ever seen. Anyway, what home? But let me fix you up with a little something—some instant cheer, you know?" Mr. Page leaned over and put some capsules into the pocket of Lee's Western shirt.

"What home" is right, Lee thought. He dug out one of the pills and washed it down with beer. Why not?

"Yeah, babes," said Mr. Page, "party. Here." He gave Lee a twenty. "After you get through here, go take a shot at the slot machines. But don't bet any more than that, right? We don't want you to lose anything serious."

"Oh, right," said Lee. He moved downstage to where Jango and Baxter were hacking around, singing "Check, Baby, Check" and dancing obscenely.

"My turn," said Lee, and they went off so he could do his sound check.

He looked out into the theater filled with little tables set up in semicircles. Looks like a wedding reception, he thought, and laughed and then jumped back—he was always startled when he first heard his voice coming out through the speakers, it sounded so swollen and separate from him. It made him feel shy. He'd been so shy and frightened, he'd had to get drunk as hell the first time they did the show, and he'd been more or less drunk ever since. He started sweating as the men up on the catwalk aimed spots at him. They always had different lighting for him because he was bigger than the others. He squinted and went through his poses, singing lines for the sound check. The band took their places and swung in with him for a few bars of "Suspicious Minds," and then he was done and they started working on the band's levels.

He toured around the theater a bit, nodding to the technicians. Everywhere they went, Mr. Page hired local crews and Lee had found they were the only people he felt comfortable with. He'd always been good at electronics, ever since they trained him in the service, and hanging out with those crews the last few months he'd learned a lot. The Golden Pyramid had the most complicated system he'd seen. Up in the control booth, a fellow showed him the setup, talking about pre-sets and digital display. The show always had the backdrop with pictures suggesting what was happening in Elvis's life. Up until now they'd done this with slide projections, but here it would be computerized, same as the sign outside. Lee looked out at the stage and the fellow tapped into a keyboard and showed him Graceland all made of bits of light and then the blazing THE KING LIVES! that would come on with his finale.

He said thanks and made his way back down behind the set. Might be computers that were the brains of it, but there was a whole lot of juice powering the thing back here. Usually, he could stand behind the scrim backstage and follow what was going on, but now he faced a humming wall of wires. He knelt down by a metal box with power cables running out of it and held out his hands. Seemed like he could feel the electricity buzzing right through the air. Or Mr. Page's party pills, maybe.

Lee went through the backstage door and found his way into the casino. Bright? The place made his head whirl. He changed his twenty and the cashier gave him a chit. If he stayed in the casino an hour, he got a free three-minute call anywhere in the county.

He got a waitress to bring him a drink and started feeding quarters into a slot machine. He had a hard time focusing on the figures as they spun. He was buzzed, all right. He tried to go slow. If he made his money last an hour, who would he call?

※

When they began rehearsing in Nashville, he called Cherry every Saturday. Cherry would put on the egg timer so they'd keep track of the long distance. Mr. Page was giving a them a stipend, but he said the real bucks would have to wait till they were on the road. Lee, Baxter, and Jango shared a room, twin beds with a pullout cot, in a motel. Mr. Page drilled them every minute, made them walk and dance and smile like Elvis. They practiced their numbers all day and studied Elvis footage at night. To Lee, it was a lot like the service, being apart from Cherry and having all his time accounted for. In '68, when Lee was drafted, Cherry was still in high school—too young, her daddy said, to be engaged. He remembered calling her from boot camp, yearning for the sound of her but terrified when they did talk because she seemed so quiet and far away. Just like she sounded now.

They'd barely started on the road, trying out in Arkansas and Missouri, when Cherry gave him the axe. She'd filed papers, she said when she called. She was charging him with desertion—gone four months now, she said.

"I'll come right back tonight," said Lee.

"I won't be here. You can send the support money through my lawyer." She said she'd hired Shep Stanwix, a fellow Lee knew in high school and never did like. He'd grown up to play golf and politics.

Cherry was still talking about money, how they wanted compensatory damages. "I gave up my career for you, Lee Whitney," she said.

She'd gotten her cosmetology license when they were first married, but she'd never gone past shampoo girl. She always said it was hopeless building up a clientele out there in the country, anyway—

everybody already had their regular. Only hair she ever cut was his. She said she liked its darkness and the way it waved up in the front, like Elvis's.

"You can come along with us," Lee said, his voice breaking. "I'll get Mr. Page to hire you on as our hairdresser—he's spending money on that, anyway, dyeing us all blue-black and training our side-burns."

"There's no use talking. It's desertion and that's that."

"But, Cherry, this was all your idea."

"Oops, there's the timer," Cherry said. "Gotta go now."

"Wait—we can keep talking, can't we?"

"Save your money," Cherry said. "I need it." She hung up.

When he called back, he got no answer, then or all night. In the morning he called his mamma and she said Cherry'd been going into town till all hours since the day he left and now she'd taken everything out of the trailer that wasn't attached and moved into Bragg.

Lee went to Mr. Page—they were playing the Holiday House in Joplin, Missouri—and said he quit. That was when Mr. Page explained that Lee'd signed a personal-service contract for two years with options to renew and no way out. "Anyway," said Mr. Page, "what's one woman more or less? There's plenty of them interested in you—didn't you hear them sobbing over you last night? You were sad, babes, you were moving."

"Ain't the right woman," said Lee.

The women who came to the show only depressed him. Every night, die-hard Elvis Presley fans, women with their hair permed big and their clothes too girlish, were out there sighing, screeching, whimpering over Jango and Baxter and him. They'd come back after the show and flirt—hoping to get back their young dreams, it seemed to Lee, trying to revive what was in truth as lost as Elvis. Baxter took a pretty one to bed now and then—he considered it a right after so much time in the role. But then sometimes Lee wasn't sure Baxter fully realized he wasn't Elvis. Jango confided he found these women "too country." He waited for the big towns and went out in his punk clothes to find teenage girls who'd want him as himself. Lee slept alone, when he could get drunk enough to sleep.

When they were in Oklahoma, he got the forms from Shep Stanwix. He sent Cherry monthly checks. He had more money now than ever in his life and less to spend it on that mattered. Now and then he bought things he thought were pretty—a lapis lazuli pin, a silver bracelet made by Indians—and sent them to Cherry, care of Shep. No message—no words he could think of would change her mind.

One night in Abilene, Jango said he was going crazy so far from civilization and good radio and tried to quit. When he understood his contract, he went for Mr. Page in the hotel bar but Lee and Baxter pulled him off. Why? Lee wondered now. They dragged Jango up to his room and Baxter produced some marijuana and the three of them smoked it and discussed their situation.

"It's two years' steady work," Baxter said. "That's hard enough to find."

Lee nodded. He lay back across the bed. The dope made him feel like he was floating.

"Two years!" Jango stood looking at himself in the big mirror. "When two years are up I'll be twenty-three. Man, I'll be *old*. "

Lee and Baxter had to laugh at him.

"Thing is," Lee said, "he tricked us."

"Not me," said Baxter. "I read the contract. Why didn't you?"

Lee remembered Cherry's hand on his shoulder as he signed. Remembered Mr. Page saying what a sweet Miss Liberty she made. And he felt Bax was right, a man's got to take responsibility for his mistakes.

Baxter passed the joint to Jango, who sucked on it and squinted at himself in the mirror.

"Mr. Page is building something up here," Baxter said. "What if we were quitting on him all the time and he had to keep training replacements? As it is—do you know he's hiring on a steady band? They'll travel in a van with the equipment while we go in the car. And he's upgrading the costumes. Not long, he says, till we'll be ready for Vegas. It's like what Colonel Parker did for Elvis."

Jango swiveled his hips in slow motion in front of the mirror.

"'Colonel Tom Parker was a show-biz wizard,'" he quoted from his part of the show. He laughed. "Page wrote that. 'He guided me. And I—'" Jango's voice deepened into Memphis throb —"'I came to look upon him as a second father.' Shit. Isn't one enough?"

"My daddy died when I was a boy," said Lee dreamily.

"Mine's a money-grubbing creep," said Jango. "Just like Page."

"Course, Elvis should have broken with him in the sixties," Baxter said. "That was his big mistake—he kept doing all those movies exactly alike because the Colonel was afraid to change the formula. No, at the right moment, you've got to make your break."

Jango snarled at the mirror. "I'm gonna save every dollar, and when I've got enough I'm going to rent the best recording studio in L.A. and sing till I get Elvis out of my throat forever."

⚹

Lee circled quarters through the machine till they were gone. He hailed a waitress and while buying a drink asked her the time. Four o'clock here. It would be suppertime in Tennessee and darkness falling. Darkness never reached inside the casino, though—there were no windows, no natural light. Could you spend your life here and never feel it? He went and turned in his chit and they let him into a golden mummy case that was a phone booth.

He dialed his mamma. When she heard it was him, she went to turn down the pots on the stove and he was filled with longing for her kitchen. So far off. She exclaimed all right when he told her he was calling from a Las Vegas casino where he was to perform that night, but he could tell it didn't mean much to her, it was too strange.

The telephone glittered with gold spray paint.

"I only have a minute here, Mamma," he said, "so tell me straight—how's Cherry?"

"She was out here the other day. Kind of surprised me. Listen, Lee, you coming back soon?"

"I don't see how I can. Is something wrong?"

"It's Cherry. I know you're legally separate and all, but I don't think she's as hot on this divorce as she was. I was talking to my friend at the grocery, Maylene, she said to say hey to you—"

"Thirty seconds," said the casino operator.

"Mamma—" Lee's heart was pounding.

"Well, I mentioned Cherry stopping by for no good reason and Maylene said it's all over Bragg that Shep Stanwix dropped her to chase some country-club girl and—not that she deserves you, honey, after how she's acted—but maybe if you get back here right now, before she takes up with anyone else—"

Lee fell into a night with stars in it. When he came to, he was slumped in the golden mummy case and the line was dead. A lady from the casino leaned over him. "I'm fine," he said, "I just forgot my medicine." And he took a pill out of his pocket and washed it down with the last of his whiskey.

The lady was tall and half naked and concerned. "Is it heart trouble?"

"That's right, ma'am," said Lee. "My heart."

⚹

They ate dinner in their suite, at a table that rolled into the living room. The hotel sent up champagne in a bucket, for Talent on Opening Night. After they knocked it off, they ordered up some more to have while they got into costume in the mirrored dressing room off Jango's bedroom. Jango was ready first, in black jeans and a silky red shirt.

"Uhwelluh it's one fo the moneyuh," he sang into the mirror, warming up. "Uhwelluh it's one," he sipped champagne, "one fo the moneehah," He looked sulkier every day, Lee thought.

Baxter leaned into the mirror opposite, turning his head to check the length of his sideburns, which weren't quite even. He plucked out a single hair with tweezers. Beside him on the dressing table was a tabloid he'd picked up that had a cover story about how the ghost of Elvis got into a cab and had himself driven out past Graceland, then disappeared. Baxter read all this stuff for research.

"Uhwelluh it's two fo the show, damn it, fo the showowwhuh," sang Jango.

Lee, who was drunk but not yet drunk enough to perform, confronted his costume. Hung up on wooden hangers, it looked like a man he didn't want to be—the vast bell-bottoms, the jacket with shoulders padded like a linebacker's, the belt five inches wide and jewel-encrusted. The whole deal heavy as sin. Lee sighed, took off his shirt and jeans, and stepped into the pants. The satin chilled his legs. He wrapped a dozen scarves around his neck to toss out during the show. He held out his arms and the others lifted the jacket onto him. The top of the sequined collar scratched his ears. He sucked in his stomach so they could fasten the belt on him, but just then Mr. Page breezed in, all snappy and excited.

"You know who we got in the audience tonight, babes? You know who?"

They all just looked at him.

"Alan Spahr!" he crowed. "I'm telling you, Alan *Spahr*. The Dealmaker!"

Baxter said, "What kind of deals?"

"Hollywood deals, babes. Hollywood. The Emerald City. We're talking moolah, we're talking fame, we're talking TV movie. What's this, champagne? Yeah, let's have a toast here." He filled their glasses. "Las Vegas to Hollywood—westward ho, babes, westward ho!"

"The Emerald City," said Lee.

The champagne was cool and sour. He poured some more and flexed his shoulders.

"Listen, man," Jango said. He still held Lee's belt in his hands. It flashed in all the mirrors. "I am not going to Hollywood. There's no way I'm going to play Elvis where anyone I know might see me."

"You won't be playing *in* Hollywood," said Mr. Page. "In fact, if we make this deal I'm going to see to it that the script is expanded—you know, do the whole life, filmed on location. Might even find a child, you know, to play Elvis at six, seven."

The poor kid, thought Lee.

"But a TV movie is on everywhere," said Jango.

"You betcha." Page drank champagne.

"I won't do it." Jango sneered. "Sue me—I don't have anything to lose."

Page leaned close to him. "Oh, no? A lawsuit lasts a long, long time, babes, and I would own all your future work if you quit me. Any albums, any concert tours, I would own your damn poster sales, babes, get it?"

"Mr. Page," Lee said, "you don't need me and Jango for a TV movie. Baxter is the real talent here. On film they can do everything with light and makeup—Baxter can go from twenty to forty, can't you, Bax?"

Baxter looked up from his tabloid and said, "I know I could do it. It'd be my big break, sir."

"Babes, I can see you wouldn't be anywhere without me," said Mr. Page. "That there's three of you—" and he gestured at the mirrors where, small in his white suit, he was surrounded by ominous Elvises— "that's the whole gimmick. The three stages of the King. And with a TV movie behind us, babes, this show could run forever."

⁂

The show was on downstairs. Lee had finished the champagne and switched to whiskey. He had to find the right drunk place to be. The place without thought. Like in the Army. Which he never thought about. Stay stoned, don't think. He checked the clock—lots of time yet. He was in full costume, ready to go. Lee avoided the mirrors. He knew he looked bad. When he was young, he was dark and slim—like an Indian, Cherry used to say. Cherry had loved him. Cherry—better not think about Cherry. Where were his pills? In his shirt, on the floor of the dressing room. He tried to bend, but the belt cut into him, stopped him. He had to kneel, carefully, and then, as he threw back his head to wash down the pill, he saw. Who was that? Down on one knee, huge and glittery, his hair dark blue, his chest pale and puffy, his nose and eyes lost in the weight of his face. He looked like nothing human.

He had to get away. He took the service elevator down. It was smothering in there, but cold in the corridor, cold backstage. Sweat froze on his chest. Jango was on, near the end of his act. Off stage left, Lee saw Baxter talking to Mr. Page. He started toward them, then stopped.

Baxter had Mr. Page by his bolo tie. He pulled him close, shook him, then shoved him onto the floor. Baxter moved through the curtains, going on just as Jango came off with a leap, all hyped with performing and sparkling with sweat. Mr. Page was on his hands and knees, groggy. Jango did a swiveling dance step behind him and kicked out, sending him sprawling again. Then Jango saw Lee, shrugged, snarled, and flashed past.

Lee came forward and Mr. Page grabbed onto him and helped himself up. The old man was flushed—his red scalp glowed through his puffed white hair. He pulled at the big turquoise clasp of his tie and squawked. Baxter was singing "Love Me Tender." Lee shushed Mr. Page and led him behind the back wall, where the music was muffled. Page kept shaking his head and squinting. He looked dizzy and mean.

"I got contracts," he said. "There's nothing they can do." He started brushing his suit—dust smeared the white cloth.

Lee held out his shaking hands. "Look—I can't go on."

"Oh, babes, you're a young man still," said Page. "You just gotta cut down on the booze some. Listen, I'll get you something that'll make you feel like a newborn child."

"When I get too old and sick to do this, will you let me free?"

"At that point Baxter'll be ready for your job. And Jango for Baxter's." Page patted his hair.

"And you'll find a new kid."

"That's the way this business goes, babes. You can always find a new kid."

Lee's heart was pounding, pounding. He had to look away from Mr. Page, at the wall of wires, lights, power.

"Yeah, kids are a dime a dozen. But I'll tell you what, babes," said Mr. Page, "you were my greatest find. A magnificent Elvis. So courtly and screwed-up. A dead ringer."

Lee looked away, listening to the noise of his punished heart.

"A dead ringer?" He remembered the first pills Mr. Page handed him, just after Cherry—don't think about Cherry—and Lee knew he would die, would die as Elvis had and never again see his wife, his mother, Tennessee.

"Magnificent," said Mr. Page, "we gotta get that look on film! It's gorgeous, it's ruinous—I tell you, babes, it's practically tragic."

And Lee struck him, with all his weight and rage. Mr. Page fell onto the metal box where the power cables met. Lee bent over him, working fast. Green sparks sizzled around them.

Onstage, Lee was doing the talk section of his last song, "Are You Lonesome Tonight?" He was supposed to get lost, say what he liked, then come back into the lyric with a roar. "Tell me, dear—" he murmured into the mike and remembered Cherry when she was just out of high school. "You were so lovely." Wrapping a towel around him with a hug before she cut his hair. "And I know, I know you cared—but then—" Oh, what went wrong? "What went wrong? You sent me away—"

He stood still and looked out at the people sitting at little tables like they were in a nightclub. Well, it is a nightclub, he remembered, a hot spot. And he laughed. "Watch out." He shook his head. "Gotta get straight," he muttered and saw tears on faces. "Don't cry for me," he said, "she's waiting." And then the song came back to him as it always returned, the band caught it up, and behind him the wall of light blazed and then ripped open with a force that cast him out into the screaming audience.

⁂

Breakfast was cheap here. Even in the diners they had slot machines. Lee drank black coffee and scanned the newspaper. He read how Liberace's ex-chauffeur had plastic surgery to look more like Liberace and about the tragic accident backstage at the Golden Pyramid. The manager of the "ELVIS LIVES" show had been caught in the electrical fire caused by the new computer system. Now, days after the accident, the newspaper was running follow-up stories about past casino fires.

The first day or so, there had been investigators around, in and out of their suite, but they mostly left Lee alone. He'd been onstage during the fire, when the finale display overburdened the wires, causing a short and an explosion. And there'd been so much emphasis on how complex the system was, digital this and that, no one imagined a hick like Lee could understand it. Even to him, his own quick work seemed now beyond himself, like something done by someone else. Lee supposed the other two thought they'd contributed to Page's death—left him woozy so he passed out backstage and got caught in the fire. But they accepted the explosion as the dazzling act of some god of electricity looking out for them. The second night, when Baxter came in with their contracts, they ripped them up without a word.

A new three-Elvis act was opening soon—Mr. Page had owned *them*, but anyone could use his gimmick. Baxter was staying on in Vegas—he'd pitched himself to Alan Spahr and they were talking about cable. This morning Jango was heading west, Lee east. Wasn't everyone better off? Except Page—better not think about Page. Already he seemed far back in time, almost as far back as things Lee'd done in the Army. Anyway, Lee blamed the pills. He'd sweated himself straight in the hotel sauna and meant to stay that way.

Lee paid for breakfast, picked up his old leather valise, and went outside. This early, you could smell the desert. The sun showed up the smallness of the buildings, their ordinariness squatted beneath their flamboyant signs. Lee stuck out his thumb and began walking backward.

The trucker who picked him up was heading for Albuquerque. At the truck stop there, Lee drank some beers and hung around till he found a ride through to Memphis. He had resolved to cut back to beer only until he saw Cherry again, but in the middle of the night in Texas he felt so good, heading home, home, home, he wanted to stay up the whole way and bought some speed for himself and the guys who were driving him, and knocked it back with some whiskey the driver had. Home, home, home, they tore along Route 40, through the darkness, listening to the radio. When Elvis came on, they all sang along.

"Hey, Lee, you sound like Elvis. Look a little like him, too," the driver said. He nudged his buddy. "What do you think? Have we picked up Presley's ghost?"

"Naw," said Lee. "He's dead and I'm alive and going home." Sipping whiskey through the night, song after song, he felt so happy he just sang his heart out.

TWENTIETH
CENTURY DESIGN

1

1963: I'm fifteen and ready all the time to be bad but nobody gives me a chance. On a summer day when just breathing makes my mouth water, here I am in my grandmother's bedroom, wrapping her purses in tissue paper. All her pocketbooks click shut. Black patent leather, navy suede, bone, white kid, black straw, brown alligator, green alligator, two dozen purses, stiff-sided and clipped closed and prissy as she is.

They have to be packed because she is moving to an apartment, because Grandpa has run off with the teller at the drive-up window at his bank. She'll be his new wife, in a new house, when he gets back from Nevada with his divorce. I have some pictures he sent from out there, of himself in a white cowboy hat, posing like he's in a gunfight. He looks tan and cute and I'm on his side completely. I only hope I don't have to wait till I'm fifty to get free of my family.

Mom and my grandmother murmur in the kitchen. Mom is trying to get her to travel, so she won't be here for Grandpa's return, but of course Mom won't say that. She says it's Grandma's obligation to see how Uncle George and his wife are doing out in Honolulu. Duty, obligation. They talk in a Catholic language that drives me nuts. Earlier this morning, when we were wrapping china, I used the word "divorce" and my grandmother said, "The church doesn't recognize divorce."

"Recognize it," I said, "this is it." Mom called me a big mouth and stuck me in here, hissing that I ought to be considerate.

I do feel sorry for my mother who is seven months pregnant and suffering. I've heard her say she's been caught in the middle ever since she came upon Grandpa holding hands with the teller in the park. I wish I had seen that. Up till now I thought he was dull, living in this house where the air is gloomy green from the high shrubbery, eating pot roast every Sunday, playing contract bridge and golf, smoking a cigar at his glossy vice-president's desk at the bank, slowly going bald. The idea of him holding hands in the park is thrilling.

I finish the purses and start packing up the gloves. Gloves, purses, shoes, hats, everything spotless and matched, that's what it takes to be a lady. The last thing I want to be. I wish I were in the park. I like to sit on the swings and watch the older high school girls, the tough ones in flats and tight skirts. I am studying them, their intricate dances, their slang, their discussions of deep kissing. I want to wear soft breasty Orlon sweaters like they do. I want to carry a beat-up vinyl sack full of brushes and mascaras and pale lipsticks and hairspray, want to dig through Chiclets, loose change, cute pens, nail files, teasing combs, E-rase, to find, under the cigarettes, in with the photos of all my friends in a plastic holder, ooh, at last, my locker combination written down because I can't remember it. I want to be dumb but oh so busy. I want to sit on the park merry-go-round screaming *no no no* as the boys push me too fast, whirling in an ecstasy sure to lead to others.

But I'm Elizabeth Doherty. Ask anyone—a too-tall girl in bermudas and blouses from Best's and loafers that smell of proper leather. I'm a little too good at diagramming sentences and can't think of any to speak when a boy gets near. Though I plan to change—when school starts, I'm going to have a new name. In July I wanted to be Beth, Beth's soft and sweet, but now I've decided the wildest is Liz.

Now Mom calls me to lunch, which they've laid out on the back porch because the dining room is full of boxes. My mother lies on the chaise lounge, her round face pink, sweat on her upper lip, her belly big inside the flowered muumuu Uncle George sent her. Grandma sits up slim and straight, wearing a beige linen dress and an organdy apron. What a thing to wear when you're packing up because your life has fallen apart. She nibbles a sandwich. Cream cheese with pineapple and walnuts on Boston brown bread, cut into quarters. Lady food. I fill a plate with sandwiches and devilled eggs, pick up my iced tea, and plunk myself at the far end of the porch on one of the uncomfortable wrought iron chairs.

Mom says, "Grandma is going out to visit George and Rikki for a few weeks."

I smile at her. How'd she pull it off? "That's great, Grandma." I chew my sandwich, looking at the faded hydrangeas. The grass badly needs mowing.

They discuss Uncle George, who stayed in Hawaii after he got out of the military, married and became a student at the university. George used to be wild but "the Marines straightened him out," Mom says. He and Rikki had an infant that died, a year ago last spring, and now everybody worries over her.

"When she has a new baby, they'll be all right," Mom says.

Grandma snaps, "She'll never forget."

"No, of course not." Mom's thin fair curls, I notice, only make her face look rounder, more apologetic.

"You always love the dead the most," Grandma says, "because they can never hurt you anymore."

There. That's the kind of amazing thing Grandma says. Morbid Victorian Catholic stuff. Mom looks like she's about to cry. She'll be teary tonight, and Dad will rub her feet, and then he'll take on even more work at the insurance agency. "Just lay low," he tells me. I once heard Mom say she got married to get away from her mother, but it didn't work.

Mom likes to think she's more modern than Grandma. When I was eleven she told me Grandma had never mentioned menstruation, so that when her first period came she stayed in the green and black tiled bathroom in this house for hours, afraid to ask for help until she decided she was bleeding to death. "I don't want you to be ignorant like that," she said to me, then handed me a booklet entitled "Growing Up and Liking It" and left the room.

Since Mom isn't so wildly modern as to actually discuss sex with me, I've looked at books on anatomy in the library. I've read of the glands of Bartholin, where the woman's excitement produces a fluid, but this knowledge, though scientific, is still vague. It's 1963, I am fifteen, ready all the time to be bad but nobody gives me a chance.

Grandma brushes crumbs off her apron into her hand. "Elizabeth, would you like to come, too," she asks pleasantly, "to Hawaii?" She flicks her fingers and all the crumbs go back onto her plate.

"Well, but school starts in another week," I say. I look at Mom. She is licking cream cheese from the edge of a sandwich, giving me no signals. This must be part of her plan, she must have persuaded Grandma taking me was an obligation. I study the fierce print of the muumuu, trying to measure having to be with my grandmother against going somewhere this bright blue and scarlet, the farthest place in America from New Jersey.

Meanwhile Grandma is saying she can speak to the principal and explain this is an educational opportunity. She can pull it off, I know, picturing her in his office with her gloves, hat, bag. I get up and go over to her, saying thank you, and we place our cheeks side by side without touching and make the sound of kisses, as ladies do.

2

Notre Dame is beating Navy, 49-0. We already know the outcome. Notre Dame will win, 56-7. When the game was played yesterday, Uncle George won ten bucks on them. The game is only now being shown in Honolulu, though. Film has to be flown in. This is before satellites are ordinary, before signals are bounced around the world. Exotic places really are far off. To me, it's as if Hawaii is in a different relation to time, something I've felt since the plane trip. When we landed, I changed ages, became adult and interesting to George and Rikki, who called me Liz right away when I asked them to and, despite my grandmother's insistence on Elizabeth, keep saying Liz. They ask me what I think, about civil rights and nuclear war and rock'n'roll. I have no opinions about football, but Uncle George is a fanatic and I enjoy sitting with him, our feet up on the industrial wire spool living room table, watching day-old sports, knowing how it will come out and seeing the players struggle all the same.

Grandma, washing dishes on the other side of the breakfast bar, says she doesn't see how we can stand it, isn't it boring, but I try to explain that it's really more interesting. "It's subtle, Mom," George says. I'm looking forward to saying that to my mother.

George and Rikki are wild. They have friends of every racial combination, they walk around barefoot at home, drink beer and laugh and tease each other. Their principal foods are Wiki Chicken in a Bucket and ice cream. The second day they ordered in Wiki Chicken, which Grandma eyed as if she'd like to cook it again to make sure it was sanitary, she offered to make the meals from then on. Tonight we had pot roast.

George and I watch the final scoring drive, which is brave and sad for Navy, and then we all go outside to eat dessert in the tiny garden. Everyone praises the view: Diamond Head to the left and houses spilling down this hillside toward the hotels of Waikiki. But what I have been watching for a week now, from the bench under the plumeria tree, is the boy in the yard two below us. The beautiful boy, who is blond so bleached it looks silver, who wears jeans cut into shorts and faded Hawaiian shirts, is restoring a pink and white Studebaker. Uncle George says cars are expensive here and so I imagine the boy has found his as a wreck and worked on it ever since. Tonight he lies under the car, stretched so his shirt is pulled up and I can see his tan belly. The effort he uses to wrench something shows in his legs.

My grandmother sits beside me on the bench and hands me ice cream. Chocolate chip mint, Grandma's favorite, the coolest flavor. She puts a spoonful in her mouth and then pulls it back out, one thin layer of ice cream gone. She gets three tastes to a spoonful, sometimes even four. I go crazy at her restraint. How can she do it? Her mouth must be cool. Me, I dig in, I eat it quick, I ask for more. My mouth is hot all the time, like Honolulu.

Uncle George goes back to study Philosophy in the living room—Grandma and I have taken the bedroom that was his study. Rikki wanders gracefully around the garden, watering the hibiscus and picking some of the strange small bananas that taste like strawberries. I love the way Rikki looks. She and her friends have this style I call Pacific. Japanese, Hawaiian, Filipino, Irish, they wear eyeliner tilted up at the corners and hair smoothed back into French twists and slender dresses with mandarin collars and side fastenings, made of Hawaiian cotton or brocade.

Rikki's wonderful job is to sit all day drawing necklaces and earrings which curve in front of her on dark blue velvet. The day I went with her she showed me how to use charcoal to create the shadows and highlights that make you want the baroque pearls in her pictures more than the real things.

Although Rikki works and never wears gloves or hats, only a lace mantilla to Mass, I can see that my grandmother likes her. With her, Grandma seems almost relaxed. Now, having finished her ice cream at last, she takes off her Italian high heels with the long pointy toes.

Her feet, in stockings, have bandaids on the heels and her toes twist into each other. Today, she walked all over a restored native village in those shoes.

"Elizabeth wears the same size I do, 7 1/2," Grandma says, and Rikki tells me to try them on. When I walk in them across the patio, my toes are jammed forward and I can feel my balance change. My belly sinks. My hips get difficult. Grandma and Rikki laugh. I go back gratefully to my loafers. Grandma puts her shoes back on and the wrinkles deepen around her mouth. She snaps open her purse, which is behind us on the table, and then snaps open the leather cigarette case and uses the lighter—snap snap snap—and inhales one of her Kools. I smell menthol.

I can hear the transistor radio of the boy two gardens down, playing "Runaway." Two girls walk by and speak to him and he lights their cigarettes. They walk around the car with him and then all three of them get into it. Their laughter blends with the gathering darkness of the gardens. This happens almost every evening—girls come by in ones, two, threes, and get into his Studebaker. What goes on then I guess at.

They send me inside to use the bathroom and I hurry into my nightgown and kneel by my cot so I can be believeably finishing with prayers if my grandmother comes in. The first night here she terrified me by asking to listen to me pray. I could hardly remember the words.

I am in bed pretending to be drowsy when Grandma enters the room. She takes her shoes off and gives the little sigh which begins her ritual. Then her earrings come off. Her ear lobes are red and flaking, pressed flat by the fanged clamps. I've tried them; they begin to hurt after a minute or two and in ten I have to pull them off.

She wrenches her arms around to unzip her dress and I wonder if she misses Grandpa at this moment. She wears tailored dresses or Chanel-shape suits, over a full slip, over a long girdle with garters that clip her stockings. When she gets these off and is down to her long bra and full nylon panties, her body is marked by creases from the girdle, and yet she's thin, with a trim attractive shape. Her skin is a white the sun never touches.

She gets into her embroidered Barbizon gown before she takes her bra off. Then she sits at the table which is Uncle George's desk. Some of her things are lovely—the crushed satin bag she keeps her hosiery in, the sachets that make me sneeze at their smell of sleeping roses, the crystal jars with silver tops that hold the creams she puts on. Sitting in front of her travel case, looking into its mirror, she strokes lotion up her throat, over her square jaw, onto her cheeks. Her face glistens with grease when she's done and she leans forward and uses her tweezers to pluck out the whisker that grows on her chin. Every night she winces, every afternoon it's back. She takes her hairpins out and puts them into an ivory box and gradually her dark hair falls around her, thick hair my mother envies.

Grandma kneels by her cot and says her prayers, silently, with her silver rosary wound through her fingers. She goes around the beads every night, three times, for the Sorrowful, the Joyful, the Glorious Mysteries. What does she pray for? Why isn't she in Nevada going after Grandpa?

She gets into bed. I can tell she is awake. I hear her blink. I have heard her crying some nights; she sniffs in, in, in, and sighs. I have heard her reach for her rosary and start over, lying in the dark, and I know she believes that if you fall asleep while telling the beads, the Virgin Mary will finish the story of Her motherhood for you.

3

In the spring of '69 I am twenty, in college. Only one year more, I think, and I'll be completely free.

I come home for Spring Break with the flu and spend the first day lurching into the bathroom. I'm there, sitting on the cool tile floor waiting to be sick in the middle of the night when the call comes: my grandmother has had a heart attack. My parents get back from the hospital at dawn. When I speak to Mom, she says, "Leave me alone. My mother is dead," and cries.

I can't understand my grandmother. She lived alone, never acknowledging the divorce, worked selling Better Dresses in Muir's, never travelled after that trip to Hawaii. Dead at fifty-seven. Not that old when he left—why didn't she pick up and go on, kick free of a bad deal. That's where I think my friends and I are smart. I'm on the pill, I sleep with my boyfriends—usually they last about three months. When I feel bored or trapped or hassled, I break it up. I'm certain there's someone else more interesting ahead—why should I make do? And if some guy dumps me first, well, there's a bad week or two, but no hard feelings. If we wouldn't have been happy, then what's the point of clinging?

I'm excused from the wake because I'm sick. Around noon on the day of the funeral, feeling empty but better, I creep downstairs and see the dining room table extended to its full length, covered with a vast spread of casseroles and cold cuts. My grandfather is there, setting out more food. He has been looking after my five year old sister and took her with him to pick up the hard rolls and fresh rye, which he is slicing. He is always tan now and a sporty dresser; today he wears his golf cap and a yellow cashmere sweater. His second marriage is a happy one, and his wife and my mother have evolved a relationship which is more than carefully warm. He gives me the heel of the rye. I tear it with my teeth, enjoy its resistance. I taste the salt and caraway voluptuously, almost giddy as the bread transforms the hollowness of my body, and then I get, just for a flicker, the trueness of death, not just my grandmother's, but my own.

My grandfather takes pickles from a jar, transfers potato salad from plastic to china bowls. Right now they are burying a woman he lived with for more than thirty years. Since their divorce, Grandma dragged the words "your father, your grandfather" into her talk as if to touch the pain, but he never mentions her. Surely he must feel strange—but I don't know any way to ask this. We put out mustard and butter. He leaves before the mourners return from the cemetery.

A few days later my mother begins to deal with Grandma's belongings, many of them still packed since 1963. When she comes home she hands me a packet of my letters to my grandmother from college, bound with a thin green ribbon. She kept them in her bedside table, a bundle of rose notepaper she gave me, about two dozen dutiful letters with hardly a word of truth in them.

Within a few years, my grandmother all but disappears from family conversations. The sad fact is that everything is easier now, no more juggling times of visits on holidays, no more going to church to keep her happy. This is how we deal with death; we close ranks, we build a new picture of the unshakable present.

One Saturday night in 1981 my mother phones. I am in Paris, in bed with a man who buries his head under a pillow and groans when I say, "Hi Mom." She tells me my grandfather has had a prostate operation and they found cancer in the testicles.

"Tsss," I exhale, the sound of sympathetic pain. I am silent, thinking what to say.

"The testicles," my mother says, "that's where the sperm is manufactured."

Something in her voice makes me ask, "Mom, do you know *where* the testicles are?"

The man beside me looks up at that, and grins, and holds his in his hands, clowning.

"More or less," Mom says.

I say, "That's the balls, Mom."

She says, "Oh," and then, "tsss."

The man in my bed is waggling around obscenely and I don't want to laugh so I say, "Cancer," and he winces and gets out of bed.

In 1982, when I am out in L.A. selling Deco furniture and trying to make a go of it with an impossible guy, I drive up to visit Uncle George. Divorced, in A.A., he pursues tranquillity in Zen Buddhism and loses his temper in traffic. He wears a beard and shaves his head, but from the shadow of hair in the back you can see that otherwise he would be bald in the same pattern as his father. George teaches something called Future Studies and is on the governor's panel for the earthquake. He lives with his girlfriend, who is a year or so younger than me, in a tiny apartment from which, if you lean out the kitchen window, you can see the Berkeley hilltop house Rikki got in their divorce. Rikki, who supported him through his Ph.D. and had two kids, found a team of women lawyers and, as he says, "picked him clean." His girlfriend tells me about a time when he was still married, when they were sitting in her car at a stoplight and Rikki walked past. She pounded on the windows, screaming, until they drove on.

Yet when I deliver my mother's request that he come east to see Grandpa, who is going through chemotherapy, George cuts me off, saying he can't forgive what his father did to his mother. To keep myself from pointing out the resemblance, I reminisce about our visit to Hawaii. George tells me that one day when we were there, he walked into the bathroom, thinking it was empty, and found me standing, fully clothed, in the shower stall, crying. "You said, 'Jesus, can't I get any privacy anywhere,'" George says in a good imitation of my teenage voice. "And I recognized that here was someone who felt just as trapped and miserable as I was."

I ride the bus from Manhattan every weekend in the fall of '83, because my grandfather is dying from the cancer, which has spread into his bones. I sit with him in the afternoons, to give my mother and his wife a break. One Saturday, while we watch college football on TV, he says he wishes he hadn't gotten remarried two hours after his divorce came through, out in Reno. "I should have been a free man for at least a day," he says.

Later, in the hospital, when he is looped on drugs, he asks, clearly, "Dear, when are the Petersons coming over?" I look at my mother, who shakes her head. Outside she says, "Oh God, my mother and father used to play bridge with them, thirty years ago."

After his death, I am home one day with my mother, sitting in her pine kitchen, drinking iced tea, when she tells me that among his belongings were documents which show that her parents had to get married. "Had to"—she gives the quiet phrase its middle class horror. Irene Kiely was 16, Charles Anspach 17. They married, he gave up college, took a job as a clerk at a bank. The baby lived only briefly. She was christened Elizabeth, the name of my grandmother's grandmother.

I look at the old certificates, their fine paper hardly touched by time, the handwriting on them elegant. I try to picture my grandmother as the girl in trouble, Irene Kiely.

My mother says she's so angry she could spit. I ask why. "Because she was a hypocrite, because she was so pious, because she never let me get away with anything." My mother's voice soars through the house, full of late rebellion.

I feel oddly pleased by the baby's name. "That's right," Mom says, "she suggested it before you were born."

I think, that's why she took me to Hawaii, why she saved my

letters, I replaced the lost child. Did she love me, then?

My mother says, "It must have been a secret reminder, all the time, like a hairshirt."

Now my mother has lived longer than her mother and reached sixty, which doesn't seem old to me. My dad's nearly retired and Mom's started a shop, selling silk flower arrangements in old baskets. She has forever the round pink face of someone trying to do things right, to please more demanding people. Aren't the difficult people gone? I ask, but she points out that I am difficult. My little sister is a married woman with a bank job and a toddler, while I keep taking off to parts unknown in hope of learning something new.

I have turned forty, forty-two, my God it goes so fast now, forty-five. Sometimes I wonder who I would have been if anyone had trapped me into a narrower path of ritual and duty. Not that I want that; I just wonder. My friends and I complain that there are no good men, but we don't really mean it. We like to have our escapades, and then get back to work.

I go home as often as I can manage. My mother gives me my grandmother's things: her fur jacket, some miniature antique pitchers that have to be dusted all the time, a set of silver grapefruit spoons, pale green waterglasses. I was trained as an art historian; I write and edit books on twentieth century design; I know better than to like these things so much.

When I'm giving a talk in San Francisco, Uncle George comes and takes me out to dinner. He describes afternoons when he was a boy, sitting with his mother in their dim house, the only noise the peas dropping into a bowl as she shelled them, moments, he says, of absolute contentment.

"Contentment for you," I say.

He laughs, "You're right. Maybe her life was creepy. But she didn't complain."

We each have a version of her, I see. To my mother, she was a liar, to George, a martyr. I like to think of the girl who must have been wild, once. And the discipline with which she hid herself.

George tells me he's through with younger women. The problem is, he says, they're younger. He has started dating his own ex-wife. Rikki paints, she teaches, people tour her gardens. "She's neat," he says. "She's feisty. She's the most interesting woman I know."

I'm nearing fifty and beginning to be distinguished. Elizabeth Doherty, you may have heard of me. I buy, in vintage clothing stores, at auctions, Chanel suits and old designer dresses. I am vain about my figure. One hair grows from my chin—it appeared when I was forty-seven—and when I pull it out I laugh and call it Irene.

4

We have been in Hawaii nearly three weeks. In Nevada my grandfather has received his divorce and remarried. Grandma has taken me on a bus ride around the island. We visited a perfume factory where we got samples of pikake and white ginger and a big bottle of carnation cologne which my grandmother keeps in the refrigerator. We toured the Mormon cathedral, the Little Grey Church of the missionaries, and a Buddhist temple which was gorgeous, like all the junk jewelry of the world melted together. It's September, but the weather hasn't changed, it's warm every day, and each afternoon there's a light shower and then rainbows hang in the air.

Sunday, after Mass, Rikki takes us up to Punchbowl, a cemetery in the crater of an extinct volcano. There are no headstones, only squares set flat into the ground, so it doesn't seem like a cemetery at all. Grandma and Rikki stand by the plaque for the baby boy Rikki had last spring, who lived three days. I listen for facts about reproduction, but they only chat about the party Rikki is throwing tonight for her friends, so I wander off. I tell myself this was a volcano, a place of fiery life. I like to picture it surprising the experts and erupting again.

When we get home, Rikki goes out with George to pick up refreshments for the party. Grandma sits in the garden, smoking, while I stand on the table to pick plumeria blossoms to make into leis. Then Grandma decides she'll go in and take a nap.

I use the long lei needle Rikki gave me to string the blossoms, which I keep fresh in a bowl of ice water. The undersides of the petals are like secret skin, tender as lips, and touching them makes unknown parts of my body heavy and warm. My grandmother has left her navy blue church-going purse on the picnic table. I open it, take out her lighter and a cigarette.

I light up and stand at the edge of the yard. The Kool's menthol makes an icy burn in my mouth, nose, throat. I cough, yes, but soon my throat is numb and I try to aim the smoke out in a thin stream. Then with my left hand I cup my right elbow, the way my grandmother does, and I feel how poised and safe this stance is, with my arms on guard, the cigarette held with two fingers in front of my face.

I look into the yards below me and the beautiful boy, bending over his toolbox, looks up, smiles, sketches a wave. I wave back with my cigaretted hand. I go inside and use Rikki's cream eyeliner in the bathroom, tilting the lines up at the corners orientally. I spray myself with chilled carnation cologne and head down the hill.

5

Lizzielizzielizzie his tongue darts in and out of my mouth *lizzzlizzz*. The afternoon's brief rain falls on the roof of the Studebaker as we kiss in the back seat. He has some blond name, Greg or Dennis, I'm so nervous I've forgotten it already. He smells like car polish and Coppertone. I'm dizzy from holding my breath— it seems impolite to breathe when you kiss—and astonished at the reality of his mouth and hands. No one in my family touches, for us the air around each other is enough, and so his hand running up my bare arm is bold, rude, overwhelming. I feel the kind of nausea you get on amusement park rides, a deep uneasy excitement. I've gotten this far by smiling and saying yes and answering questions, my name and where I come from, and by admiring everything about the car, its steam-cleaned engine, its ivory plastic steering wheel, its white leather interior with secret pockets. I'm not sure what to do next and when I try to sneak a breath around the corner of his mouth he stops and leans back.

His face is flushed yet calm. After all, girls come and kiss him for his surfer looks and pink car all the time. He talks easily, telling me about the best beaches and how someday he will go to Australia. I realize I am already bored with him, though not with kissing. His mouth is rubbed red and there's long blond down on his upper lip. I want to touch it, and when I do he is on me again, *lizzlizz*, and his hands reach my breasts. He pauses—there must be something I'm supposed to do. I flex to make them bigger. I'm interested as he squeezes, all I want to do is find out more, he can touch anywhere he likes. He figures this out; he pushes me down on the white leather seat, palms circling my hipbones. I am trying to decipher his shape, pressed against me, moving to feel more, and then I hear, "E-liza-beth."

My grandmother's voice rings out right over our heads.

He has pulled his hands away from me.

We look out the back window of the Studebaker. My grandmother is leaning over the hibiscus bushes. The rain has ended and the rainbow rises out of Uncle George's yard. "E-liz-a-beth." Now she looks as if she's calling up into the plumeria tree. I can't tell if she's spotted me or not.

I'm already half out of the car. He smiles and stretches. I say I have to go and wave a kiss at him and run back up the street.

As I come up the sidewalk, she is standing just outside the front door. She wears her Italian high heels but her robe hangs open over her slip. Her hair has tumbled down in back. She looks warm and mussed and beautiful. It's as if I have caught her. I think, she could have kept Grandpa, if she really wanted to.

"I was just talking to this kid down the street"—I say "kid" to throw her off. I wish her to say nothing and I get my wish. She gives no warning, no threat, no information, just suggests that I get cleaned up before supper. I feel transparent when she looks at me and yet I hope she is too innocent to imagine what I've been doing. Too prudish, isn't she?

In the bathroom I wash off the eye makeup, relieved Grandma didn't comment on the long smear across my cheek. Then I step into the shower stall and kiss the back of my hand, planning how I'll manage tongue and breath next time. I know I'd better go slower, learn more. My body feels fluttery and deprived, and I surprise myself by bursting into tears. I'm crying, calming down, and then my uncle barges in. I step out of the shower and say with all the disdain I can manage, "*Je*sus, can't I get any privacy *any*where?" and stalk out.

Tonight we are having what Aunt Rikki calls a hen party. Uncle George has gone out, Rikki's girlfriends are coming over, and we're going to watch the Miss America pageant.

Grandma wears her new fitted Hawaiian dress—not a muumuu, it's called a holoku. Rikki fastens a gardenia in Grandma's mass of dark hair and introduces her as Irene Anspach, as if she were a friend. The house fills up with female voices. Rikki and Grandma have made canapés—little skewers of pineapple and ham, smoked oysters on Ritz crackers. I put them on trays ringed with my plumeria leis and pass them around. Drinks are mixed in the blender. I get gingerale and am being a good girl, inconspicuous, trying to take in the way Rikki's friends cross their legs and the little Hawaiian phrases they sprinkle in, *pupule* for crazy and *pau* for done or enough. I have decided to study sophistication. I think I'll try out the name Lisa when I get back home.

The women tell stories. Rikki tells one about how George, when they were first married, got drunk and led all his Marine pals, drunk too, in a parade through their bedroom while she was in bed. George played the trumpet. The women laugh and shake their heads, even

Grandma.

We turn on the TV, though it's not quite time. The June Taylor Dancers fill the screen. My grandmother, with her dark Manhattan and her cigarette, sits next to me, looks closely at my face. She says, "Rikki, you can see just how Elizabeth's eyebrows should go, a bit off here and here, see?" and the others fuss around, and Rikki brings her makeup kit.

Leaning near, Grandma touches me with the cool tips of the tweezers. It gives me a quick electric pain each time she plucks, but I hold still for fear she'll stop. I concentrate on the smell of carnation, the powder clinging pink on her nose. I clench my jaw the way she clenches hers and never twitch as she "clears out" the middle and "raises" the arch.

She holds up a hand mirror to show me. My skin is red and blotched. Rikki gives me cold cream to soothe it, and I dab it on, take that sting too. "Oh," the women sing, "how it opens up your eyes."

Then we all settle back with our drinks. I want to thank my grandmother and ask her what she has seen, in my eyebrows, of who I might someday be, want her to explain the mysteries of beauty and pain. But she's closed off again, eating chunks of pineapple in ladylike bites, poised over her napkin so no drop spills.

Bert Parks comes on and they begin the Parade of States. I know who will win, Donna Axum of Arkansas; it happened last night. I saw her in today's paper. Grandma has insisted we not tell her. She doesn't want to ruin the suspense. But it isn't ruined for me; I like the way you can see as they go by—*Miss New Hampshire! Miss New Jersey! Miss New Mexico! Miss New York!*—all the girls shimmering with hope.

MACY IS THE
OTHER WOMAN

T he night before my trip, when I see Emily at a party, I can tell she doesn't know.

She seeks me out among the drinkers in the kitchen and again on the back porch beside the keg, and I let her tell me how she went to Washington last week to help Jay move into his new apartment. She describes the moon rocks at the Smithsonian, a Ukranian restaurant, a homeless woman who chained herself to the White House fence. I agree with her that this separation will be worthwhile if the job gets permanent. "Already," she says, "it's made Jay steadier. He can't come home for the Fourth of July because the Congressman needs his position paper."

Despite myself, I speak to her with a certain confiding tenderness. Even tell her selected low points of my love life. We split the last of some flat champagne, support a motion that men can be bastards, and agree that the two of us should get together soon for lunch. "But I'll be out of town for a few days now," I say.

Sometimes you wonder how you got so tough.

In the morning I'm out early on the road. It's hot by nine, too hot for breakfast. The sun on the black upholstery brings out a whiff of the vinyl when it was young. I itch in new jeans from the outlet store—oh yes, I still have that impulse to buy something to please, but these days I am broke, I buy cheap.

The bridge I'm supposed to take is under repair, and I follow detour signs roundabout into D.C. with Jay's map open on my lap. I park in the garage he said was the best deal, find the right building, buzz. And buzz. Jay said he'd be at home and on the lookout.

Finally an old woman comes up from the pool and lets me in with her, through three locked doors. Even the elevator requires a key. When she lets me off on the eighth floor, I feel my trustworthiness has been visible to her. I sit against Jay's door, breathing the air-conditioning that smells like the cool cellar where I played as a child, among the poles that held the house up and the clean bleached sheets.

Jay gets off the elevator with groceries. He looks alarmed. He hadn't thought I'd make such good time. We don't kiss; I don't really want to. I go into the bathroom, calling to him that I'll take a shower. In the mirror, I see my wind-teased hair, my one red shoulder. It takes most of the motel-size bar of soap to get the indigo dye off my stomach. I put on a summer dress that wraps and ties, held by one ribbon worked through a series of slits, and come out rubbing baby oil on my legs.

Jay lives like a squatter in this one room apartment. White sheets drape the glass doors to the balcony. He owns two folding chairs, a boom box, a tiny TV. There's talk of a bed he can get from a friend, but for now an open sleeping bag must do. The hairs on his arms, on his chest, are as harsh as the fibers of rope, but I like that. He never does quite get the dress off.

The dishes are Emily's, two Blue Willow plates, two cups, two saucers, and she bought him the set of six steak knives when she was here. Otherwise he has a bag of plastic forks, a water glass stolen from a restaurant, an aluminum double boiler of his mother's. Pepper and salt in little packets. Iced tea going bad in an apple juice jar. The freezer developed some sort of mold before he moved in. Emily scrubbed it but it still smells wrong. I scrub it too. He cooks the steaks on a hibachi on the balcony. We eat on the floor with the TV on, watching murder in a different part of town.

After dinner, we go out for a walk. The once raunchy waterfront has been cleaned up and you can sit on benches and consider the lights of lobbyists' yachts. We visit a shop that sells tables made from the hatches of sailing ships, ashtrays that were once torpedoes. He hints that he could use a table, but I say I'm not supposed to be the one who buys him things. Besides, I'm broke. He gets himself some pillows made from batik sarongs.

He offers me paperbacks to read—Jerzy Kosinski, Chekhov's plays, an Agatha Christie I've read before. I skim it to see what it's like when you already know who's to blame. Jay is reading Vaclav Havel. We sit side by side, naked on the sleeping bag, propped against the new pillows. Jay is somber over police informers, false arrest.

When he goes to work, he leaves me all the keys. I lie by the pool in the too-small side-tied bikini I haven't worn all year. I'm convinced that I've lost weight since yesterday. I tell myself I should look on this as a vacation. The water in the pool is as hot as the sky. Nothing evaporates. In the afternoon, I find white silhouettes of knots and bows on my hips as my sunburn develops.

I like the mild voices of the young men on the FM station. This one sounds so gentle, his consonants enunciated like the least whisper of fingers on the strings of an acoustic guitar. He tells you what you'll hear next, and then what, and then what after that.

It reminds me of Jay's tone, the evening when he first approached me, after we had played together in a ragtag softball game. He'd been with Emily three years and never faithful. But he loved her, he said, make no mistake. Loved her so much he couldn't breathe unless he cheated. He said we'd be passionate, and then we'd get tired of that, and then we'd be friends. No love. He promised me we wouldn't have that pain.

Well, it appealed to me. I consider myself post-devotion. I have begged and been begged, tossed men out, taken them back. It's tiring. And one morning you wake up alone, in a state you never planned to live in, with a dumb job and debts. Surely you can learn to change. Or so I tell myself.

He comes home early and we watch part of a movie, one of those low-budget, foreign-made children's films. The mouths of the grown-ups move out of time with their warning voices. The wolf wears mascara. The little girl, coming upon him in the woods, stops on her spot. Plainly she's seen wolves before. Her fear is pure flirtation. Jay turns the TV off and we enact the story. His wolf, with the sleeping bag pulled up to his chin, growls in Russian. I flatter the size of his eyes, his ears, his teeth.

He has two grips of flesh at his waist. My hands skim by, preferring to ruffle the hair on his chest. In this sort of affair there is no need to learn to like the bad parts.

I notice that he always chooses my left breast.

I find that I am falling into trances. I stare for half an hour at the hunting print, blue on buff, of the sleeping bag lining. I look at the Today Show and notice that the pattern of fronts on the weather map, two loops, makes a W, like the monogram of Weather. Several times, in the middle of sex, I catch myself admiring my own leg, tan and slender, up in the air. I like my ankles. I wiggle my toes to see the light glint on my toenails.

During sex we compliment each other. Your skin's so nice. Oh that feels good. Delicious.

Afterwards he says, "Macy, are you awake? Want some tea?"

It has the effect of an intimate remark.

Jay spreads documents across the parquet floor. He is working hard, he says, on the position paper for our congressman. Jay plans to be the expert on business in Eastern Europe, the reintroduction of competition.

I pick up a page and read: *We must proactively reward the entrepreneur who heretofore may have been viewed as a state criminal—*. Another sheet breaks down the stages of post-Marxist distribution of sausages.

I joke that he should get people to call each other Entrepreneur instead of Comrade. "Good day, Entrepreneur. Entrepreneur, wherever did you get such a beautiful, formerly criminal fur coat? Woowee, Entrepreneur, that's a fine post-Marxist sausage you've got there."

He chases me around the room, telling me that I am not a serious person.

I reply—we are sprawled across statistical reports—that he is certainly proactive.

On the third evening, he says my legs are prettier than Emily's. Sensing danger, I am quiet. "She loves to cook," he says. "When she was here, she made me a peach pie."

I tell him I'm not the one who's supposed to cook him things, but then I send him out for fresh bread and while he's gone I make pasta with clam sauce, the best I can do with only two pots. I cannot find a pie tin, nor a rolling pin. I wonder whether Emily brought them with her and took them back home or whether she fooled him with a store-bought pie. Or, of course, he might have lied.

While he sleeps, I prowl the apartment. In the bathroom cupboard there's a half-filled box of tampons. Slender regulars. And Emily has left other supplies: baby powder, a new loofah. I get hot water going in the tub and squeeze in a little of her bubble bath— French lavender. Then more; let Jay take the blame.

I sit in a tubful of sweet astringency. Emily has tea-colored hair and a veil of freckles. She looks like a shy woman, but each time I have met her, at the farmer's market, a couple of parties, she has been the one to speak to me. I remember the afternoon I saw her in the park, carrying a bunch of irises and a bakery box tied with red string, and I thought, that's the kind of woman I might be friends with.

That was the day after the softball game she missed because of work. The one Jay walked me home from, talking about Russian literature, I remember, following me up the stairs saying something about Turgenev, seeing me—oh yes, safely—to my furnished rooms, to my old chenille bedspread from home on the fold-out couch. Even as we got undressed, we discussed humiliation in Chekhov. No love, he offered me, and I accepted.

And then, next day, Emily stood in leafy shadows, holding irises, and said she hoped I'd play again, when she'd be there. She told me Jay had said, the night before when he came home, that he thought I had a pretty decent swing.

The Fourth of July, both Jay and I have headaches. But tomorrow I'm supposed to leave, so it's time to be tourists. He takes me to the Smithsonian to see the moon rocks, which are just rocks after all. I tell him Emily thought so too. He looks disgusted.

We join the jammed folk festival at the Mall. This year the theme is the Mississippi. At the foodstands they are frying catfish. The temperature is 98. The humidity is 85 percent. Jay tries to leap aboard the Huck Finn raft as it crosses the Reflecting Pool and falls in. As he wades out, wet to the waist, he yells at me that he did it on purpose, stop laughing. He looks foolish, but, I think, Emily loves him. Would she see him as endearing now?

On the steps of the Lincoln Memorial, teenagers flirt. We stand for a while below Lincoln's knee. Lincoln is a comfort. We feel great-browed, far-seeing, for a moment. Then out again, into the sun.

Hot, I drink beer and feel hotter, sun burning my shoulder blades, sweat down my sides. My acetate sundress is spongy. Sitting on wooden bleachers, we listen to old Mississippi fiddlers. Around us, miserable children wail. My heart beats fast, too close to the surface. Jay kisses me and at first I don't want to, it's too hot, but then I figure what the hell and kiss back, let us melt, our skins slick against each other, his hands gliding my arms, his smell a pond, and when I touch, inside his cut-offs, his damp thigh, he groans, "*Emily—*"

We stare at each other. Maybe seconds pass, but I have time to see how his face will broaden with age, how he will lose the gloss of youth but gain sad power. His hair hangs in wet points. In his surprising light brown eyes I see some fury I don't understand—is he angry I'm not Emily? Or is this how he looks at her?

Then he gets up in a kind of panic, like he'll run away, and I try to follow, but I'm stuck to my seat. My dress has dissolved, fused with green paint. I yank and rip free, peeling splinters from the wood.

He is standing with his back half turned, looking miserable. He says, "Oh God, I'm sorry, Macy—"

I don't see how to tell him that I liked it, being Emily, swimming into his thirst for her.

I say, "Look at my dress—it's ruined."

He says, "I knew I was with you, Macy, really—"

"It doesn't matter." I make him stand behind me and look at the damage.

He says he'll buy me a replacement—as if the dress is his fault, as if I tore it because he called me Emily.

I say, "Of course not."

He says, "Believe me, Macy, I'd be glad to."

I say the dress was cheap anyway. He gets a cab and takes me to a vacant lot where people sell vegetables, junk, and antiques. I find a vintage strapless in strawberry silk and let him force me to accept it.

I point out that there's really no reason to keep calling me Macy every five minutes.

We get iced cappucinos and walk. Now that he's bought me something he feels better. "Jeez that was embarrassing," he says.

"Just better watch that you don't do it the other way, with her."

He shakes his head.

"Do I remind you of her?"

"You have the same shoes," he says.

"Shoes?"

"Yes—not those—your pink sneakers. She has identical ones, I noticed it a long time ago, at softball. Do a lot of women have them?"

"Sure. Why—do you have to sleep with everyone who does?" I laugh.

"You're strange," he says.

I suck ice through the straw. "How am I strange?"

"Don't you want somebody of your own, somebody you come first with?"

"Are you criticizing me for sleeping with you?"

"I suppose, in a way." He shrugs.

We're walking down a back street, holding hands, having this conversation. I sway between feeling almost close and sensing that we could fight any time, our words like claws.

That evening we bring the lawn chairs up to the roof of the apartment building, so we can watch the fireworks with the other tenants. We wait for the darkness to deepen enough. Jay complains that from here the noise will be diminished, just puny pops. He tells me about the fireworks of his childhood, the times he sneaked across the park and hid behind the firemen who got to light the fuses. He describes the reverse side of the ground displays, the whistle as the skyrockets went up, the bits of burnt paper falling on him, and then, delayed, the Boom Boom BOOMM! he could feel in his stomach.

I agree, I too miss the great explosions.

Others on the rooftop give us drinks. I have a beer, a rum and Coke, some cool rosé. I know I have lost weight. The new dress floats around me. Jay holds my hand while he talks to strangers about his work. He recounts how in Hungary they used to make underground copies of jazz recordings on old x-ray plates. "Those are the people," he says, "we must find and build on."

I say, "That's funny, nobody has that much respect for jazz lovers here."

When the group laughs, he sighs. The first skyrockets go up, white screamers. After a minute he says to me, "You know, Emily told me about your mockery. She said you were someone who had figured things out."

"Is that why you went for me?" I ask lightly. "Her recommendation?"

"That's right," he says. "I was afraid you'd get to be friends." He smiles charmingly.

"Maybe we will," I say.

"But if you do," he says, "I'll tell her about us."

I have to laugh. "Aren't I supposed to make that threat to you?"

He shrugs. "She always forgives me. But you—" he squeezes my hand, lets go— "she won't forgive you."

I look at him against a sky full of red chrysanthemums. They turn into blue whirlybirds. His face is locked. I see it's true, this was his plan.

I say, "I have to admire your dedication."

"Don't get me wrong, Macy. It's been a pleasure." He kisses my cheek softly and moves away.

I concentrate on the fireworks display, holding my eyes wide to let the after-images burn. I picture myself on a porch with Emily, laughing, with our feet up. Both in our pink shoes. Telling stories about the amazing ways of men, confiding all our foolishness. I know Jay's right—this would have happened. I think of Emily at parties, at the famers' market, in the park, seeking a friend. I wonder if I can find a way to warn her—and whether any warning ever works. Smoke drifts my way, and bits of charred stars.

When I look around after the final extravaganza, I don't see Jay, so I fold up our chairs and carry them downstairs.

He is on the telephone, talking baby talk. He rolls his eyes at me.

I look for a place to get out of their way. I go out on the balcony and shut the sliding door. At first it scared me out here, but now I'm used to it. There's music from the roof. Aretha.

He taps the glass door, mouths the words, are you all right?

I shrug, I nod. He blows a kiss. I hear him say, "Yes, of course, of course I do. I do too."

I look over the edge at the traffic tie-ups far below. The night smells like catfish. I find I am dancing with my arms folded around me, tangled in my own embrace.

THE FORMER
STAR CARLSON

How I Got Engaged

I kicked Tommy Falcon out at the end of May in '91. Tommy had never formally moved in, but was sleeping over most nights and accumulating stuff and just getting more and more comfortable, which was courtship as I knew it. And then that night, as we lay in bed cooling down from sex, he got up and I heard him moving through the dark apartment, bumping something in the living room and kicking aside a stack of papers in the hall. Then came the *screek* of the freezer door fighting its build-up of frost. Here I was still floating with all my senses dilated, but did Tommy think of that? I got up and found him standing with the fridge open, vapor pouring dreamily around him while he ate the last of the ice cream out of the carton with a tablespoon. I had, at the sight of him, a naked blond guy with a waist-up tan, a stab of unfamiliarity—*what is this man doing in my kitchen?* Okay. So I hollered about how greedy he was, and careless, but what I really meant was how dare he make himself at home.

I got so jangled, I grabbed him by the arm and before he thought to resist I'd slung him out onto the back stairs. He sat there laughing and saying how nuts I was while I tossed out his jeans, which he hopped into, and his boots and shaving kit, guitar, amp, effects box, and what clothes I could find in my washpile. He didn't try to come back in. Just told me I was making a big mistake. I slammed the door and locked it and held my breath until I heard him stomp downstairs, heard his car start and putter off.

I threw the ice cream carton out—nothing in it but vanilla crystals. It had been in the refrigerator nearly a year. I pried free some ancient burritos and two boxes of baby lima beans and then I began to defrost.

Stevanne heard the fight, of course, since she lived just below me, and when I went by around noon she had Tecate and limes in the fridge and we spent a couple of hours on her porch saying He was useless and You're better off and Why are men so, tossing our empties on the lawn for emphasis.

I hadn't slept much, nor eaten anything till Stevanne brought out some chips and salsa, midafternoon, and by then I was thoroughly drunk. I felt good, though, light and truthful, sitting in her green wicker rocker in the shade of the live oak.

Stevanne was my landlady. She inherited this big house with the double decker porches all around, elegant but shabby. I'd been living there three years, since I came back to Houston after my stint trying to make it singing in L.A. I still got some club work around town and over in Austin, picking up money between times as an office temp. Back when Houston was flush, Stevanne was a promoter of arts events, things like an opera about Davy Crockett. Then oil fell, banks failed, and art sponsors lost their sense of adventure. So she'd been temping, too. She'd had to drop rents, and even so the apartment next to mine had been empty for six months.

Our friendship was based on the mutual admiration of women who look nothing alike. Stevanne, five years older than me, was tiny, stylish, with hair chemically shocked to show her commitment to the experimental. I, well, I have the height and bones of my Swedish-German ancestors but the coloring and curves of my Mexican grandmother Estrella, for whom my daddy named me, though my mother quickly translated it to Star, like the Star of Texas. My music? I had clippings said I was feminist, I had clippings called me cute, I did blues, folk, rockabilly, zydeco, a little bit of everything—is that anything at all? Stevanne said I lacked priorities, in music as in my relationships. She preferred the distance of affairs with married men.

From the other side of the hedge came the voices of alcoholic women working in the garden of their halfway house in the June heat.

"This time next year," one said, "we'll have those bees. I hear they're coming up from Mexico now."

"Those killer bees?" said another. "We'll have to get a big old net." Then the two of them sang "Inky Dinky Spider" for some reason and laughed. I thought of them over there, sober, while here we were, drunk. I thought of myself as Inky Dinky crawling up the spout again.

"Stevanne," I said, "I'm just not getting anywhere."

"You'll meet someone new in no time. You always do."

I shrugged. "Then I'll just have to start over with the talking and trusting and that. I'm too tired of it."

"Take it easy for a while. What's the rush?"

"I feel—behind," I said. "Thirty-two and never married."

"Married is not so great. Believe me, Star," she said. "I've been there."

"That's what I mean." I blew across the beer can, took a slug, blew again. The note was lower. "Everybody's been married. Even my brother—they split up, did I tell you?"

Stevanne pulled her much-bleached hair up in two choppy handfuls. "Are you saying you want to be divorced?"

"Right. See," I said, "I don't want to *be* married. I want *to have been* married."

This was a great revelation to me. I went off to the bathroom. Why do you always feel drunker when you go to the bathroom? I looked at myself in the mirror, touching those two tiny lines that started bracketing my mouth last winter.

When I came back out, the light had changed. Oak leaves rustled and lifted. The little foreign guy who had recently rented the garage apartment was biking up the street fast, trying to beat the rain.

Stevanne had put out some cheese. She sat folded up tiny on the chaise lounge. "So you want to get married and divorced, do I have it now?"

"Yes ma'am."

"Done," she said, waving her hand like the fairy who grants your wish knowing just how much trouble your choice is going to bring.

She called out to the new tenant, who brought his bike up on the porch. He had a face with no flesh to it, all jaw, cheekbone, brow, and then his hair jumped from his head in a fierce wave. His head seemed too big for his body, which was dressed in space-age neon elastic bicycle clothes. Stevanne introduced him as Basil Essaloonis, a post-graduate student in computer science and architecture. "I am an ergonomist," he told me. His accent rolled the word around impressively, so I nodded like I knew what it meant.

"Basil is from Russia originally," Stevanne said.

"Not Russia—Estonia. By births Estonian, by citizenship I belong to Curaçao, Netherlands Antilles. I am wanting to be American."

"Sooo," Stevanne said, "the other night Basil was telling me he needs to marry an American to get residency so he can stop going to school and make some money. Star is thinking she'd like to get married for a little bit. I think you two should get together on that—then when Basil gets his green card you can split right up."

He gave Stevanne a funny look, I thought. She just smiled and ate some cheese.

I said, "You want to marry me?" I was laughing.

With dignity he said, "You were helping me a ffery great deal if you do this."

And I said why not and Stevanne dangerously drove us down to the marriage bureau in the rain and for twenty-five dollars cash Basil got a license. We needed two forms of ID. Basil had a passport, credit cards, student identification from two universities, while I only had my driver's license and, after a long search through my purse, my tattered social security card. The clerk explained there was a seventy-two hour hold. This was Friday, so we agreed to marry Monday afternoon. "Good, a June wedding," Stevanne said.

On the way home we stopped at a Circle K for beer and charcoal, because Stevanne said if Basil was going to be a Texan he'd have to learn to cook out. Before the burgers were grilled I went upstairs to my place and called my mother out in Sealy to say I was getting married.

"Don't tell me, Star. I don't want to hear it. I've been burned," she said, "too often."

Rhythm and Blues at the Reception

I wore an orange minidress to my wedding. Basil wore a blue suit. Stevanne had a temping job, so we rounded up the old gent who had a folk art shop on his side of the first floor and one of the sleepy nurses from the third and took them along as witnesses. Was I nervous? Did I hesitate? Not really. Maybe if Tommy had called— but Tommy didn't call. Basil was jumpy. His eyes were sunk in dark circles and the bones of his skull protruded more than ever. I asked if he was okay, just before we went in to the J.P., and he said, "I had neffer before so sleepless nights as now, at new beginning." There was something touching about him and I felt proud to help. It made more sense than anything else I'd done recently.

Over the weekend, Basil had reconstructed the tumbled brick fireplace out back. For our reception he was barbequeing chicken for his friends from the U. of Houston and Rice. The tenants came, too, and the old gent gave us our first wedding present, an outline of Texas made from barbed wire.

Basil's friends clustered around the keg in the shade of the carport. It was in the 90's and, of course, humid, and the alcoholic women next door were singing a draggy version of "Both Sides Now." The hotter the weather, the more beat the music has to have, I say. I went up the back stairs to my place and carried my tape deck onto my porch, where it overlooked the back yard. I put on Etta James as loud as she went.

I sat on top of my part-stripped pine chest, going through a shoebox of tapes to line up more tunes. Looking down, I saw

Stevanne pull in under the rippled green plastic roof of the carport. She greeted Basil by the barbeque and began handing out paper plates. I was thinking how when my daddy was alive he'd horrify my mother with descriptions of my wedding, a real Tex-Mex party where all his friends would dance with me and pin money to my dress, when a tall man stepped up beside me and said, "It's not too late to back out."

He had on jeans and a blue dress shirt, black bolo tie. His hair was dark with some gray to it and he wore it long, tied back neatly. His left ear was strange, extra big and an odd pink. I judged he was flamboyant because he wore an earring in it, little turquoise stud.

"I beg your pardon?"

"I'm Robert Brandenburg, a friend of Basil's and his lawyer. Your lawyer, too. For the immigration?" He sat down in the cut velvet armchair that had swallowed a century of dust. I looked apologetically at the porch, still littered with last fall's leaves, and the ugly grass rug I'd been meaning to throw out. The other end, which belonged to the empty apartment, was stacked with sets from a show of Stevanne's, a bayou *Midsummer Night's Dream.*

Robert Brandenburg seemed to be concentrating on his dark blue tooled cowboy boots. "I sure don't mean to imply that you and Basil aren't seriously intending this marriage to last," he said, "but you should know that the I.N.S. may not believe it. I explained to Basil when he came by last week that they'll try to prove the marriage is a sham. They get lots, done for money of course."

"Well, that's not the case here."

He held his hands up— "I didn't say it was. But you ought to know that if they decide against you, they'll kick Basil out and they could prosecute you for fraud. So if you have second thoughts, well, I can get you out of it quickly while he's still got a student visa."

"Why would they decide against us?"

"You and Basil will have to document your life together and you'll likely be questioned, separately, to see if your answers match."

"What kind of questions?"

Robert Brandenburg did a sharp clerk's voice: "Mr. Essaloonis, what does your wife keep in her top bureau drawer?" Then he transformed himself into Basil—stuck out his jaw and gave a tired glare. "Of course, is her nighties." He looked at me. "Mrs. Essaloonis," the clerk again, "what's in your top bureau drawer?"

I was laughing. "None of your business."

He got up and strolled through the open door into my bedroom with me after him. He opened the top drawer of the battered dresser and raked through the clutter, cataloguing, "Belts, scarves, pennies, Bandaids. Set of Allen wrenches. Box of unused Christmas cards, tampons, what's this? An Astros program. You like baseball?" Tommy liked baseball. "Vanilla perfumed oil. And a Cinderella watch. Basil has his work cut out for him."

I said, "Now we're married, of course, we'll reorganize."

He looked skeptical.

"We'll build in shelves from floor to ceiling in the living room," a plan I'd long had, "and put all my—and his—books and instruments and important stuff there. That'll make space in here for Basil's dresser. And whatever Basil wants. We haven't discussed it in detail."

I knew it sounded thin. The light through the lace curtains was going lavender, softening the messiness of the room, but not much. Robert Brandenburg wandered around, looking at the postcards stuck to the mirror and the old screen window I'd hung up to hook my earrings through. He ran his fingers along a row of feathers and beads.

"Guessing won't do," he said. "I told Basil to stop by and pick up the list of questions I've compiled. Even legitimate spouses— like you and Basil—can have difficulty with them unprepared." He sat on the unmade bed. "And a couple other things you can do. Make sure the wedding is announced in the paper. Do you have a bridal photograph?"

"This was a sudden decision."

"Well, get one, if you can, in something that looks more traditional than that, fetching though it is."

"Sounds like the I.N.S. is pretty old fashioned."

"Oh, they are," he said. "Patriarchy is sentimental. That's their weak spot. Remember that. Otherwise there wouldn't be a loop-hole at all."

I went over and sat in the windowseat, my favorite place, where I could be surrounded by lace curtains and look right into the live oak where it grew in over the side porch. Tucked in the corner was my old mandolin, the prettiest thing I owned. I said, "Basil and I didn't promise we were going to inspect each other's dresser drawers, down there today. I mean, all we did was get married, we didn't have to say a thing about the structure of our homelife."

Robert Brandenburg looked at me, then away. Seeing him in profile, I realized who he'd been reminding me of; he looked like Thomas Jefferson on the nickel—same thick hair pulled back, same carved Anglo face. "Interesting theory," he said.

"As far as I can see, all that we're really bound by law to do is not marry anybody else, isn't that so? Like you have a right to marry till you use it up. I know people, married, who never speak to each other. Live in different cities sometimes—musicians do."

"Dangerous," he said. "The government might get to thinking you could live in two different nations just as well. And, shoot, there goes your loophole. Nope. The nation state is sentimental and that's a good thing. In the law's eyes you are united, that is, a unit, and so you shouldn't be divided. Can't have two countries."

"Or two minds?"

"I believe that's grounds for divorce."

Don't think I didn't know what was going on here. There was attraction going on here. At one time—all my life so far—I'd have gone with it. I'd have leaned over to old Robert Brandenburg and gotten him to kiss me and pretty soon he'd start sleeping over and accumulating stuff and so on. But this evening I felt different. I said, "Excuse me, Robert. I'd love to talk more. But I'm kind of busy since it's my wedding day," and went and held the door so he'd have to leave the apartment.

Of course I went right down to Basil and asked why he hadn't told me we'd have to go through a federal Newlywed Game with big penalties for wrong answers. He said he'd told Stevanne—he called her Steffana—and admitted he'd first invited her to go through this charade. And when I got her off to the side to find out why she hadn't filled me in, she apologized and reminded me we'd been polluted at the time. I resolved to give up afternoon drinking. I asked why she hadn't married Basil herself. She looked at me like I was crazy and said, "I've been married, remember? You hadn't and you wanted to and now—you *are*."

I looked over where Robert Brandenburg was eating beans and watching me. If I backed out, where would I be? I said, "You better help me through this," and she swore she would.

PORTRAIT OF STAR ESSALOONIS AS A BRIDE

A few days later we dragged Stevanne's wedding dress out from under her platform bed, where it had been since her mother dumped it on her after her divorce. Her mother had had it sort of embalmed and boxed, something they sell you with the gown, Stevanne explained. We got it out and unstuffed. The dress was an off the shoulder style, which I squeezed into with the back unzipped. It smelled like shellac and roses. Stevanne arranged a white lace piece over my head.

She'd called one of her photographer friends to take the shot and he set up lights at one end of my porch. He specialized in something he called "Distressed images," where he scratched the negatives and then overprinted and rubberstamped the finished product. We made a deal. He would do me a couple of straight prints and then he could have the image of me as a bride to distress as he pleased. He went off to work on it.

As Stevanne helped me out of the dress I asked, "What was he like, your husband?"

"He believed in fact. When we'd argue, he'd plunk down a fact and think that settled it. Kept saying he didn't deal in feelings, meaning my feelings. He himself was a swamp of feelings." She had the dress off me and right side out and was trying to fit it back into its box. I put my shirt on. "He kept stats on sex," she said.

"He once told me we'd dropped from 3.5 a week to 0.7. You know what? I think I'm going to throw this dress out," she said in a happy tone. She tossed it, box and all, off the side of the porch.

I said, "Help me with this, while we're at it," and the two of us threw the old grass rug overboard as well. I swept up the leaves, bagged them, and went down and cleaned up the yard.

Next morning the photographer delivered prints of my wedding photo. I looked demure, with well-lit shoulders. I wrote up an announcement to go along and sent them to the *Post* and out to my mother for the Sealy paper.

Questions

Basil and I filed papers with the I.N.S. and got an appointment set for our interview. Basil picked up Robert Brandenburg's question sheets, and we went to work.

I memorized: Basil Essaloonis, born in Estonia, 1947, son of a boatbuilder. When he was six months old, the family made their getaway, at night, across the Baltic, rowing. They moved around Europe—Denmark, West Germany, Holland—then leaped to the Caribbean, where they ran a small boatyard in Willemstad. Basil grew up repairing American pleasure craft. Returned to Europe in stints through his 20's and 30's to study as draughtsman, architect, computer engineer, leaving each time money ran out. Came to Houston to combine all in further graduate work in ergonomics.

What is ergonomics? The study of the arrangement of space to fit the human form. Basil had a system for designing computer workspaces to prevent ailments of wrist, neck, spine, eye. Boats are traditionally ergonomic.

One day I was out back washing my car. It's a big old LTD my mother passed on to me when my daddy died and I've been keeping it going ever since. I was doing my usual quick job with the Murphy's Oil Soap when Basil came out of his place with some bug and tar spray he used on his bike. He started working on the lower parts of the car I usually skipped. I began cleaning the interior. Every once in a while one of us would sing out:

How many rooms in our apartment?

Is our oven gas or electric?

What did I wear to bed last night?

Basil and I agreed that when in doubt, we'd say naked, which would prevent getting tripped up on costume details. We recited our birthmarks, shared scars.

Which reminded me. "How did you hook up with Robert Brandenburg?"

"He was professor at Rice. A nihilist, I think. He taught the necessities of the loophole for justice. So he does not gets tenure because conserfatiff faculty thinks his ideas are anti-legal. He sets up as immigration lawyer, an actiffist. He and I are of an age, we make friends."

"Do you know what happened to his ear?"

"No. Is brave, though, the earring, don't you thinks?"

"Yep." I tossed out the collection of diet soda cans from the floor of the back seat.

Basil spoke from somewhere around front. "What a big car. Ffery Texan, yes?"

I noticed he said it *Ticksin*, just like a Texan. "How many languages do you speak?"

"With family, Estonian. Then German, Dutch, little French, Papiamiento—island language—and English. You can understand this English?"

"Oh yes." I pulled the mats out of the car and sprayed them off.

"English is difficult," he said. "Especially the folk language."

"Like what?"

Basil leaned back from cleaning my grille and thought. Then he began to laugh, a silly laugh, sticking his tongue out and wagging it around. "The other day I haff tea with Steffana and she tells me it is herb tea let it steep. And that I do not understand—a hill is steep, a mountain, but tea? It is confusing."

"What made you want to live here?"

"My parents, efferywhere they work hard, make money, and

people are saying oh, they must smuggle, they must steal. Because they are foreign. Most places are like this, I think, but not here— here, nobody care. We don't be nosy for each other's business. Effen you and I," he said, "we study question list but if we are both American we can marry and neffer haff to."

The grunge of ages was coming off the mats. I soaped and resprayed them.

"You are good to do this for me." Basil concentrated on the Ford's yellow paint. "Steffana says you had the boyfriend?"

"Oh, well, several. You know. I'm into serial relationships."

Basil laughed with his tongue out. "This is like the serial killers?"

GIFTS

My brother showed up one morning in late July with his pickup full of boxes. Edgar lived out in Belleville, where he got married two years before this time I'm telling about. He and his wife had what seemed like a depressingly normal existence, twin recliners in the living room and movies on the VCR. Both of them putting on weight. Then she left, and he took to helping our mother with her antiques shop, driving her to auctions, doing some furniture stripping. He began to collect log outbuildings, sheds and such, some of them two hundred years old, that he bought off ranches getting sold up for bad debt. He set them on a piece of land in Sealy, his own historic village. I'd told him to move into Houston, more social life, but he wouldn't. We were close, in a wordless way.

He was quiet now, just wedged open the doors and began humping cartons up to my apartment. "What is all this, Edgar?" I asked.

He handed me a note from our mother. It said that even though my marriage was strange, it was official, announced in the paper and all, so she was sending the things she'd been storing till I was a bride. There was my grandmother Estrella's china. Great grandmother Carlson's silver. A Streak of Lightning quilt that went back in the history of my mother's mother's people in Pennsylvania. A hand-painted blanket chest, ditto. Linen pillowcases embroidered "His" and "Hers." There were cartons of my school reports and Daddy's childhood books. Some of these things I'd begged for years ago, when I first moved out on my own. She'd had them stashed in her pointy house with the piecrust trim, saved for the moment when she decided I was an adult.

"Edna," I said in exasperation.

"Edna," my brother said with love. To an outsider, our tones would sound the same.

Edgar drank some iced tea, standing in my kitchen. "Listen," he said, "I'm just giving you back the wedding present you gave me, right? The blender. Never use it. It's in there somewheres."

"Thanks." I tried to radiate sympathy.

"I guess you know what you're doing," he said, sounding like he was sure I didn't.

"At least this way I'm helping someone. Before, I used to open up my heart and then feel crowded and neglected, both, and that'd make me mean."

He nodded. He knew. I asked if he'd take my half-stripped pine chest and finish it when he got a chance. We lugged it downstairs. He hugged me and left. I considered that a good visit and I bet Edgar did, too.

Late that afternoon, I was unwrapping bits of my childhood when Robert Brandenberg showed up to remind me Basil and I had our I.N.S. interview next day. I wondered why he hadn't just phoned, but I was feeling so swarmed by memory, I was glad to have company.

He asked if I was prepared for the interview.

"I guess Basil and I know each other as well as anyone does. Except the people who really know you."

"You know it'll likely be two years before Basil's residency's granted?"

I shrugged. Basil had told me, but by then I'd memorized his life. I wasn't going to back out.

He wandered around the living room, looking at the chairs piled with linens, the stacks of books. "What's going on?"

"Wedding presents." I was teasing, I'll admit. I was sure he knew what we were up to, but I wasn't going to acknowledge it.

He stopped at the barbed wire Texas silhouette, which I'd hung over the doorway to the bedroom. "Texas is in love with its own outline," he said. "You ever notice how it's everywhere?"

"What's so odd about that?"

"Whatever you have to proclaim, you're really talking to yourself, don't you think? The border, like it was solid." He glanced into the bedroom, sighed, and faced me. "I'd like to apologize for how I acted, that first time I was here."

"What do you mean?" Which in Texan meant *I know what you mean but you're going to have to say it.*

"I meant to be helpful, but afterwards I thought perhaps I was— intrusive."

"Mmm," I said, "not a problem." Which meant, it had been, but the apology was accepted. "Would you help me with this? I should unpack it in the kitchen."

He took the other end of the heaviest carton and followed me. Boxes jammed the kitchen floor. When Robert straightened up, his head brushed against the long braid of garlic hanging from the ceiling. He looked uncomfortable, which made me like him better.

"You look tired," I said. His hair seemed more pewtery, his ear more sore.

"Lots of paperwork. I've got all these Mexican farmworkers trying to prove they've been here long enough to get the amnesty."

"My Chicana grandmother's family was here long before Texas had an outline. The Carlsons, you know, they were the foreigners. This was her wedding china."

"Pretty," he said, running his fingers over painted rosebuds.

"And these dessert dishes—" I laughed. "She used to tape a nickel to the bottom, so we'd find a prize if we ate all our pudding."

I served us ice water in jelly jars, moving aside some plates on the counter. "Sanwishes. She used to say it that way, the English word, my grandmother Estrella. Sanwishsh. I got the idea that all food was part of wishing, luck. Guess it is, when you've gone hungry. To her this stuff was important, not fame, not glamour."

"Fame and glamour—that what you want?"

"I did. Went out to California. All I can say is, they saw me coming."

"What happened?"

I thought of the many ways I'd been fooled, all through believing in myself. No. How could I trust him to laugh in the right places when even I wasn't sure which they were? "I was just lost. I came back where I know my way around. I don't think I could do what Basil's done."

"You know, anything you tell your lawyer is confidential."

"Oh, so you won't blab to anyone about my grandmother?"

"You know what I mean."

I edged over to the fridge and poured myself more ice water.

Robert said, "Who are the people who really know you?"

"What?"

"Earlier you said you and Basil know each other as well as anyone, except the people who really know you."

"I guess I meant family—although even they don't keep up. Anyone know you?"

He set his glass down carefully in the crowded sink. "Sometimes I think I'm completely transparent," he said, "but nobody's looking. Good luck tomorrow."

After he left I dug out Edgar's blender and whirled up some milk and peaches. I lay in the living room among family things and looked for a long time at my barbed wire Texas, so ferocious and intact.

Vows

What is the color of your front door?
What is your husband's favorite dish?
What was the last movie you went to see together?

The I.N.S. interviewer, Mr. Taylor, a heavyset man in his fifties, just kept writing down my answers, and I got the idea they were filming us, too, something about how stiff he sat. At the end he raised his right hand, and I had to raise mine and agree that what I'd told him was the truth.

Then he leaned close and said, "Come on, Estrella, this man is ten years older than you, he's over-educated, shares none of your interests, now, you can tell me, why did you marry him?"

"Love," I said, looking him square in his sentimental, patriarchal eye.

CORRIDO

After a day of saying Smith Klepfert Klepfert in my receptionist disguise, I pulled in under the carport and saw Basil and Robert setting up sawhorses in the yard. I took off my high heels and padded over to see what was up.

Basil said, "You are not telling me, Star, that you need shelffs, but Robert says. We just been to the lumber yard." As he said "lumber yard," he looked at Robert like, I got that right? But Robert was digging through a toolbox, frowning.

I wiggled my stockinged toes in the warm grass, feeling pleased and touched and unsure how to say so.

Basil said, "Reach as tall as you can." And he measured, with his snapback metal yardstick, my highest reach, my eye level, my bend and my crouch, so he could design my shelves ergonomically.

I went upstairs, changed into a loose shirt and cutoffs, and carried onto the porch the little bench from home, its legs carved into faces like Aztec nutcrackers. Basil and Robert had their shirts off and were drinking beer in blue glasses. I got my guitar and tuned it. The beer looked good and cold, but I was sticking to my resolution, no drinking in the daytime. Instead I sang the words: *beer in blue glasses*. Somehow they were Houston to me, the bayou air, this big, dim house. I started thinking about the corridos, storytelling songs, written after a crime, an adventure. My daddy used to sing *El Corrido de Pennsylvania*, about leaving cotton picking in Texas and going to work in the mills up there, where he met my mother. I began to make a song about how people hold on here, about dancing when you're too tired to move, eating chiles when you're crushed by the heat. About my brother collecting rough structures that last. I got lost in it. With song writing you have to try out the wrong words on your scrap of tune, till new words stick and their feeling alters the melody. I played it over and over, hoping to trick the changes out, the better ideas which must be hiding in my mind. The corrido floated over the men in the yard as they built shelves in the green shadows. I tried to match the beat to their work, make their sweat easy. I thought about how music flies outward, to reach and gather us. The men worked into the evening as the orange sun hung on, and when the shelves were done I had finished the Corrido, which was sad and somewhat silly, of Beer in Blue Glasses, the first song by Star Essaloonis.

When I played it then, straight through, applause came over the hedge from the halfway house for alcoholic women.

END OF THE HONEYMOON

Things were piling up at my place. I arranged good china in the cupboard, family linens in the linen closet, and the stuff I pulled out more than filled my mother's cartons. Early one morning on my way to work, I stopped by Stevanne's and asked permission to throw a yard sale.

"Good thought," she said. "I'll go in on it and I'm sure Basil—" Just then Basil came out of her bedroom in a blue and white kimono. His hair jabbed up more than usual.

"I hope you don't mind if I sleep with your husband," Stevanne joked.

"Just don't you hurt him." I was surprised to find it was Basil I felt protective of. Stevanne widened her eyes at me, which meant,

I'll tell you everything, later.

"We must haff discretion," said Basil. "Robert tells me it is possible I.N.S. will send inspector here for follow-up."

Stevanne said, "I've merged your mailboxes. Maybe you could keep some of Basil's things in your place, Star, so it looks right?"

"You can have the whole hall closet," I told Basil. "It's been my junk heap. I'm going to sell or scrap whatever's in there."

Basil said he would clear it out and offered to make us all flap-jacks.

Stevanne got all the tenants involved, wrote the ad, made signs. She devised a color tagging system so people could pay at the front and we'd keep track of who earned what. We cleaned out the basement; we emptied closets ruthlessly. We hauled our goods to the first floor porches, priced them, and covered them with bedspreads. Friday, the day before the sale, I had to temp, but Basil and Stevanne priced all day.

That night, I sat in on mandolin with an all-female string band at Fitzgerald's for one lovely set. They tried out an arrangement of my corrido and it sounded just right, old fashioned and new. I came home happy at 3 a.m., lay sleepless for an hour, then showered and went down to price some more. I put on Pe-Te's Cajun Bandstand softly when it came on the radio at 6:00, and Stevanne joined me, bringing coffee.

While we worked, she whispered about Basil. He's been after her for months but she'd held him off. Then one night they were watching the dissolution of the Soviet Union on TV, drinking to Estonian independence, and though Basil didn't even remember the place, hadn't been there since he was six months old, still Stevanne had been so moved, the end of occupation, brave little Estonia, well, anyway, they tumbled into bed. Now she said she worried he was too involved, but she smiled, so I knew she liked it. I teased her about finding the ideal married man.

We weren't supposed to open till 9:00, but by 7:30 people were lifting off the covers. We shooed them away while we carried the big furniture and theater flats onto the lawn, then let them at it.

For the first hour or so, I was on the side porch, couldn't tell what was happening out front or back under the carport where Basil had tables. I broke up a fight over a doorstop that wasn't for sale. A young Korean couple purchased my old dishes. A red-headed woman buying a portable sewing machine (Stevanne's, $20, a bargain) introduced herself as director of the halfway house. She said how they liked us as neighbors, offered produce from their garden.

By 10:30 business had slowed and the sun was pounding. I ran out to Woodhead with extra signs, tacked some up near the Safeway, and bought cold sodas.

When I got back, I wandered around the house dropping off drinks. The nurses were taking money at a table under the live oak. At the old gent's shop, I admired the sale display of sweet Mexican paintings on tin thanking the Virgin for her intervention in lost causes. Stevanne was inside her apartment, where teenage girls were trying on clothes.

Coming out, I studied the front steps, a social history in shoes, thick heels of one decade, spikes of another, clogs, Chinese slippers, platform sandals, aerobic nurses' shoes, purple granny boots (mine), worn blue Ryders (mine). If these tastes are so fragile, I thought, what of other attractions, how do we expect them to last? Then I decided not to sell the purple boots.

I picked them up and cruised around the side porch to see how much of my junk was gone. I found Robert Brandenburg reading under the live oak in my dusty velvet chair ($15), wearing my red Olympic five-ring sunglasses from L.A. ($4—A Collector's Item!). KPFT's Music of India was on the radio.

"I've been shopping. I particularly like this symbolic object." He held up a heartshaped eraser (50¢). "Yours?"

I gave him a soda, popped one open for myself. I sat on the wood cellar hatch, leaning back against its slant. In the Indian music I heard Texas, pedal steel guitar and Cajun accordion. I felt pleasantly giddy from lack of sleep.

He'd gone back to his paperback Perry Mason. While he read, he pinched the lobe of his left ear, playing with the turquoise.

"What happened to your ear?" I said, then, "I'm sorry, is that too personal?"

"Not at all. But it's a long story," he said and leaned back to tell it. "Happened back when I was married—"

"Star!" Basil came around the corner, skinny in neon green running shorts. "I haff looked for you. Good news! Man from I.N.S. was here already."

Robert said, "I didn't see any investigator."

"Oh yes. He ask many many questions, so I know he must be goffernment. And I convince, tell him we so crazy about each other. He effen buys some things." Good, I thought, he can't be meaning to bust us. "He buys Star's baseball gloff."

"I've never owned a baseball glove."

"Yes, sure, from the closet you tell me to clear out. And he buys pair of running shoes. He look at this—" Basil picked up a guitar strap I recognized as Tommy's— "but he decides not, was neffer worth fife bucks, he says."

Robert said, "*That* kid?"

"Basil," I scrambled to my feet, "what did he look like?"

"Young fellow, yellow hair, wears blue jeans. I think he's undercoffer."

"Basil, that was *Tommy*." I tried to picture it—Tommy finally showing up after I'd forgotten to expect him.

Robert asked what Tommy'd said, exactly.

"He asked about Star and me, our marriage. So I tell, we fall in loff when I come to liff here, we get married, we are happy as clams. He shake my hand, wish me best wishes."

I said, "I can't believe he bought his own things."

"Guess he was afraid," Robert said, "to make Basil jealous."

"Seemed like a nice guy," said Basil.

I said, "Wait a minute, wait a minute," and dashed around the porch, as if I thought I'd catch him.

Two women sat on the front steps, trying on shoes. The nurses lounged on a yellow vinylette couch marked Sold. I hollered for Stevanne and she poked her head out her front window. I asked if she'd spoken to Tommy.

"That was a while ago. He just tossed down some money and went off."

"Why didn't you tell him to hang on till I got back?"

"I didn't know you wanted to see him so much." She opened the shade wide and perched on the sill.

"Do you have any eight and a halfs?" asked one customer.

"Just what's there," Stevanne and I said together.

"My opinion," she said, "he waited till you were out of sight before he showed up. He heard you got married so fast, he figures that's how come you booted him out. Hurt his feelings."

She gestured for me to sit beside her so we could pick Tommy apart, like old times. But I kept standing. "How come you didn't explain things to him, then?"

"I didn't think that was a good idea."

"Oh? Why not?"

"Aren't you better off without him?"

"Maybe so, but why do you get to decide? You know, you have a habit of arranging other people's lives just as you please."

She didn't say anything.

"And it's a jackass thing to do. You did it when you got me married to your boyfriend in the first place."

The two customers stopped teetering along the porch to look at us.

"Why don't you come inside?" Stevanne said.

I said, "No, what's the point," in a disgusted tone I knew would hurt her.

I stomped down the steps and out into the yard. I felt jangled and dangerous, ready to fight with anyone at all. I worked along the tables, picking things up and slamming them down square, till I got over where the Shakespeare flats leaned against the hedge. I scrubbed a vintage toaster with a towel, staring into the impossible blue-green foliage.

Basil came and hovered beside me. "I am sorry, Star. I would neffer want to make difficulty for you. I will call this fellow and explain."

Men! I banged the toaster down. "That's how you all are," I

yelled, "you always think you can fix what you break, you're so careless, you waltz in here, get me into this mess, and then you take it on yourself, you—" I gasped.

"Fforeigner," he said sadly.

"No! Who cares about that?" I shouted. "No, really." I tried to hug him, but he pulled away and stood, skinny and grief-stricken, with his back to me. His hands covered his face.

I started crying. I felt horrible. I was still pissed off—but I couldn't bear having hurt him—and I was mad at him for misunderstanding—and I hated myself for getting mad—and this whole knot was something I knew I'd always dreaded: "Oh, why," I wailed, "why *why* did I ever get *married?*"

Which was when Robert Brandenburg handed me a stuffed monkey, a yogurt maker, some 8-track tapes, piling things into my arms, gabbling, "Can you make me one price for all? Do you have a bag?" It was hard to tell where he was looking in those sunglasses, like he had five eyes. He whispered, "Don't say a word," while at the same moment Basil darted past us.

I whirled to see him approach a heavyset man who stuck his hand out around a picture he was carrying. "Mr. Essaloonis," the man said. "Pardon me. John Taylor."

He was our interviewer from the I.N.S.

"Mrs. Essaloonis." He came on and shook the two fingers I wiggled free from my armload of junk.

I looked around for Robert, but he was on the porch, suddenly interested in the fit of beige pumps on one of the customers, kneeling at her feet and testing where the toes were.

Mr. Taylor said, "I just happened by your yard sale." He sounded so casual I almost believed him. He was looking back and forth from me to Basil, both of us tearstained and intense. "Fine old house. Can I, uh, pay you for this?" He held up a framed poster of an America's Cup winner (Basil's, $12).

Basil put an arm around him like an old pal and hauled him down to the cashbox.

I let all I was holding slide into a carton of curtains and moved quietly around the house till I stood in the shade of the carport, looking at my green skin and feeling scared to death.

Robert Brandenburg touched my shoulder. "You all right?"

"I think I've hollered my last. Do you suppose he heard me?"

"Of course. You were impressively loud. I guess that comes of being a singer."

"Oh God, now we're in so much trouble. Robert, what's going to happen?"

He took those stupid glasses off and grinned, my lawyer at last. "No, don't you get it? You were great. You've taught me a new tactic. Nothing's more convincingly domestic," he laughed, "than the wife blowing her top."

I shook my head. It wasn't funny to me yet.

Basil came back and gave me a hurt look. "I tell him that we are really so much in loff."

We were trying to reassure Basil, when Stevanne came around the corner with half a dozen women who carried peppers and zucchini, pole beans and yellow squash. The director of the halfway house had a farm basket full of corn. Stevanne handed me two beautiful tomatoes, heavy and warm. I knew they were fat red apologies.

I gave one to Basil, excused myself, and went upstairs.

COMMUNITY PROPERTY

I set the tomato on my kitchen windowsill. My place pleased me—it seemed cooler just for being so empty and clean. My living room was a neat geometry of shelves, my bedroom tidy, the bed covered with the Streak of Lightning quilt. I lay down for a while, but couldn't sleep. From outside came the hubbub of a growing party and the smell of lighter fluid.

I wandered out to the porch. On my side, now, there was only my nutcracker bench. But I was surprised to see, at the other end, my same old velvet armchair. I sat on the bench and watched as Robert Brandenburg came out of the next apartment, carrying a

TV tray (Stevanne's, $5 for the set). "Thought you might like some food." He handed me a bowl of salad. "I wanted to ask you," he said. "I'm thinking of renting this place, if you don't mind."

I shrugged. "I know Stevanne needs the money."

He gave me a fork, then went back to his own side, sat down to eat. We lapsed into silence. The salad was minty but had a jalapeño burn. Down in the yard someone was playing the riff from "Tighten Up" on the saxophone ($30) I accepted once in trade for guitar lessons. I hollered down, "You can have it for twenty if you treat it well."

A woman called up her thanks.

Somebody turned up the radio for the Traditional Texas Hour.

Robert said, "If I take this place, I'll be hoping to hear you play guitar, evenings. Writing songs. I liked that."

"Could happen." My fork scraped the bowl. I hadn't known I was hungry.

"I'm sorry," he said, "no nickel."

I laughed.

"So you wouldn't mind my living here?"

"Depends. I guess I'm pretty territorial," I said.

He walked halfway down the porch, then drew an invisible line beside him with his boot heel. "Well, there's the border. I can honor it."

I went and leaned on the porch railing, just my side of the line. "I thought you believed it should have holes?"

"I hope there are some."

We looked down below us where Stevanne directed some of Basil's friends as they set a scenery flat on sawhorses to make a banquet board. Basil had the coals hot and two women from next door lugged an industrial size pot of water through the hedge and over to him. The red-headed lady was shucking corn while the old gent skewered vegetables and shrimp.

"Tell me," Robert said, "why did you marry Basil?"

"I got these little lines beside my mouth said it was time."

"Quote marks," he said softly.

Close up he smelled of mint and pepper and sun. I thought

about crossing the border tongue first.

Smoke blew from the grill and music billowed, old Tex-Mex with its mix of Celt, Chapultapec, and polka. Moving to it, men mashed avocadoes. Women bopped around the yard with platters of salad, pinto beans, bread. The words complained about love, but the beat was so damned merry we grabbed each other—who moved first we've argued ever since—and danced on down and around the long porch, laughing, surprised to discover we had such a lot of room.

BEAUTY

S usan sat in her girlhood room in pajama bottoms and an old black bra, doing her pregnancy test. Not that she needed it. She was nine days late and already her breasts felt huge, swollen under her arms and strangely sensitive at the nipples. And she was so dizzy. Floors sponged underfoot. Pregnant at thirty-three from sex in a hatchback with a boy who couldn't be more than twenty-three, twenty-four.

It was 5:15 in the morning. Soon her mother would be up, filling the house with force.

She lay back on the carpet and looked up at the ranked figures of her thirty-three Barbies, each on her stand on the long white shelf, each costumed by Susan's mother in an outfit handmade to represent the year, beginning in 1959, her first birthday. From her earliest memory there they were, multiplying as she grew. When she'd complained—at twelve, thirteen—that she was too old for dolls, her mother went right on, planning, designing, sewing the annual costume exquisitely. She said, they're valuable. She said, someday they'll go to your little girl. And each time Susan left home, the dolls stayed here, waiting for her to screw up and return.

At eighteen she'd gone off to college and majored in theater arts. Her family told her this was foolish, squandering her expensive education, but she had been unable to pull away from the fascination of working on herself. She liked altering her letter *A*, saying the word *water* over and over. She turned out to have a gift for using makeup to delude people about the shapes of faces. In acting classes, she excelled at strong emotion—terror, rapture, and despair. When she landed a part, though (she played a deadly sin in *Everyman*), she found she had the necessary feeling but not the control to remember blocking at the same time. She was at her best just before the play, standing with the other actors in a circle, holding hands and opening up their throats, reciting *Bay Bee Buy Bow Beauty*.

Even with the reduced ambition of being a makeup artist, she had a rough time in New York. She walked dogs in all weathers, she stayed up late doing the makeup for a sixty-seven-year-old cabaret singer, she slept on the floor of the closet of an apartment on the Lower East Side, and finally, she went home to Maryland with walking pneumonia and slept for two months.

A nice young man came after her and brought her back to share the wealth he was picking up on Wall Street. He thought having a wife in the theater was luxurious and didn't mind supporting her while she performed with a women's group that denounced patriarchy and sports. They rehearsed often, long improvisational sessions in which they complained about their crazy, awful, lovely, wasted mothers. They performed four times at a tiny theater that was really a SoHo living room, a piece called *Woman is Liquid* in which all she did was cry. Meanwhile the stock market crashed and she and her husband stopped being able to go out for dinner and then he told her he wanted her out of the way while he failed, even though she didn't at all mind failure, even though everyone she knew failed jauntily as a way of life. They divorced and she went back to Cumberland. From her marriage she retained some wonderful luggage and bad credit.

The dot on the stick was pink, positive. Susan buried the test in her closet, snapped the light off, and got back into bed. She waited for the bad feeling: pregnancy. Panic and sweat and some grim plan. Instead she laughed. It was hilarious, delicious. Probably that was hormones. She put her hands on her belly and felt nothing. But her breasts—they throbbed, they swelled, they pressed opulently against each other.

If I stay here, she thought, it will all be impossible. I'll fight with Mom, Dad will be kind but he'll feel disgraced, and my brothers will go after the boy—the poor boy. But I could take off. Go someplace new. Jemma is out in California; she said I should visit. Santa Cruz, wasn't it? I wonder if I can find that card. I can go out there and scrounge some kind of work and have the baby. Once there's a real baby, well, what can anyone say?

She pulled the covers up to her chin and went to sleep.

On their stands, the Barbies watched over her, with their sixty-six doe eyes.

⚘

"Lazy Susan, will you get up, will you get up, will you get up," her mother sang. The shades snapped, opening the morning. *Lazy Susan*: probably her earliest memory. And who knows how much damage that did? She stretched her legs under the quilt. Her mother was telling her to get a move on, it was 7:30 already, Dad had left for work, and she had to get out to the store after she gave Susan breakfast. She really doesn't think I can get my own breakfast, Susan thought. She doesn't think I can do anything. But what does she know? She hasn't the slightest suspicion . . .

Susan drank orange juice, took a vitamin, and let her coffee go cold. For ten years she'd lived on coffee and now she couldn't stand it. She could swear she smelled chemicals in it, some taint of processing. She could detect preservatives in the strawberry jam. She sniffed through the refrigerator and chose orange marmalade—that was pure. While her mother was out of the room, watering the houseplants, she ate several spoonfuls of it and threw away her English muffin.

While her mother got groceries, Susan went through her clothes, picking out her biggest shirts and sweaters and tossing them on the bed. She went up to the attic to get the bags from Italy her husband had bought her, made of leather that only got more luscious with time. She shuffled through a stack of papers till she found Jemma's postcard with elephant seals on it, mating. The invitation was vague and there was no phone number, but they'd been room-mates at school and she knew Jemma could stand her for a few days, anyway. After that, she'd find something. She laughed again. Her own optimism seemed funny to her . . .

Then she was outside. (She kept losing chunks of time. It must be hormones.) She loaded her makeup collection, neatly packed in a set of vintage lizard travel cases, into the trunk of the Olds her father had passed along to her when she came home. He'd sweetly said it was a good excuse to buy a new car.

Her mother stormed up the driveway with a beep and jumped out to see what she was doing, crunching over the remnants of snow in the yard in her red rubber boots. It was another gray, gray, gray March day in Cumberland, wet and rusty. Susan became aware that she herself wore just a T-shirt, jeans, and leaky sneakers. But she wasn't cold at all. As she carried groceries inside, she carefully, cheerfully presented the California plan. Lied and said Jemma had called at 10 (7 A.M. out there, you know) to beg her to come right away, there was a theater job. She'd have to leave first thing tomorrow morning. That would be wonderful, her mother said, a new start. And so tonight's dinner would be a farewell. She'd have all three of Susan's brothers over, if she could get them. There was a pot roast in the freezer.

Susan looked over towards the gap in the gray mountains that led west from Maryland. Her mother babbled. It was sad, really, that she knew Susan so little, that she didn't suspect a thing.

⁂

But if I told her, Susan thought, up in her room where she was sorting and folding clothes, I'd have to explain, over and over, the boy. And how to explain that? She'd volunteered for the job of doing makeup for a small college production of *Guys and Dolls*, just over the line in Virginia, teaching a couple of sessions on the craft of disguise, thinking she could at least put it on her resumé. He'd been the one the others overlooked; that was the main thing. Hair too short and ill cut, skin poreless and transparent, changing color with each thought. No mask. The young girls didn't like that. She had shown them her greases and powders, secret mixtures and recipes for getting tints safely off the face again, and listened to their lament: no interesting guys. When she'd said, "Jeff?" they'd wrinkled their faces (messing up her work), dismissing him. Too straight, too serious. But Susan had seen his broad square back, his fine skin, and his capacity for devotion, not yet used up. The girls would rather have someone to complain of, though—and hadn't she once been like that herself?

After the show, taking his makeup off, she had covered his face in cream (he'd been one of the drunks at the mission, a character part, a complete transformation), and she'd gone in very close to take the wrinkles off his neck and—no one could see—she licked the hollow at his nape and watched the blush spread up his chest, his look of wonder in the mirror. "I like you," she'd said, matter-of-factly—it was that simple. Only then it turned out they were a pair, both living with parents, with no space of their own but cars, and in the hatchback of his she'd felt the condom split as he withdrew. It had been in his wallet, he said, a long time, at least a year and a half, two years. Disease, which was all they thought of in New York, seemed unlikely—he was so grateful and flustered. She'd forgotten to worry about this, the complication of health.

Her period had been due in two days. So the sperm had to survive time in the rubber and then clambered a long way, and the egg had lounged, holding up in her tube just enough. She knew dozens of women who had worked hard with calendar, thermometer, and drugs to do this. She felt the vanity of undeserved achievement.

※

At the bank, she nearly fainted. Once she had her money— eleven hundred dollars in traveler's checks—she wobbled outside and gasped. The air was steely. You wait, she told the thing inside her—a dragonfly, a pollywog, a smelt—I'll take you out of here to a place where the wind is a kind breath, where whales swim by.

༳

Her mother was polishing the silver. The dining room table was unfurled for dinner with her brothers. Across it her mother had thrown an old sheet. She had out the Victorian coffeepot, sugar and creamer, silver-topped cruets, salt cellars, gravy boats, gill measures from the time of Paul Revere. Her mother's was a life spent in preparation and cleanup, with too little event.

Susan took a chair across from her. "I like doing this," her mother said, defensively. (Had she said anything? Had she questioned the worth of this chore?) "It lets me sit. Lately I'm so lazy."

"You're never lazy."

"Oh, yes, I'm so lazy—" She darted out to the kitchen to turn the heat down under the soup. "So lazy that sometimes—" She stood on her chair to pull a set of candlesticks from atop the hutch. (Susan felt ill looking up at her.) "So lazy that I look forward to going to the dentist because I can just sit still in that chair and *rest*."

"You're tired," Susan said, seeing, it seemed for the first time, the circles of blue-white skin under her mother's eyes. Veins popped across the backs of her hands as she polished the coffeepot.

"This was my grandmother's. Someday when you're married— I mean, married again, really married, you know, settled—it will be yours."

Susan thought, what if I said, right now, *I'm pregnant.* How astonished she would be.

"She was a great worker," her mother said. "She used to take all the rugs outside, this time of year, and beat them. Spring cleaning, you know. She used to say, your great-grandmother, that you could tell God was a male because he rested."

Susan had heard this many times, her mother's one joke, but now she got it. She saw the long line of women beating rugs and cooking banquets, who never fully shut their eyes at night; even in pain, in illness, they were alert, ready to jump up at a child's cry. They polished, scrubbed, ran their fingers into dusty corners, ironed, while they let men strut about work. Labor. A woman's word to start with.

✳

In her room, Susan had to lie down among the piles of clothing on her bed. The Barbies stood tall on their ever-arching feet. She never played with them. Play was for lesser dolls named Tammy or Jenny, dolls who could be bashed, dirtied, denuded, who wound up bald and eyeless and beloved. Susan might touch Barbie's hair with a fingertip or fluff out a skirt, but even that could wear her, diminish her. The first one, 1959, wore the full skirt and prim blouse of a fifties housewife. For a time they followed the spirit of each year, capturing 1962 in matched coat and hat and A-line dress, a lace-edged hankie in her tiny purse. 1964 wore mod dress and go-go boots, and 1967, Hippie Barbie, an India-print skirt with flecks of mirror. Her mother had put flowers in her hair, had made the tiny tie-dye T-shirt. She had strung red beads and researched the daishiki for 1968's Black Barbie, a mocha Barbie really. Her features were the same, of course, the nose no one could breathe through, the egret neck. Then her mother had moved from public history to private, reproducing Susan's riding habit from the year she'd been horse-mad, her prom dress, her off-to-college outfit of wool skirt and cowl-neck sweater, Barbie's knitted on size AA needles. The wedding gown—the real one was in the attic somewhere, but Barbie in hers looked fresh and hopeful. Virginal. But then, Barbie would stay intact through anything. Susan looked down at herself, so interestingly unintact. In August she would be thirty-four and five months pregnant. What would her mother make? There could be no maternity Barbie. Barbie could never change shape, thicken. Barbie, of course, was very, very careful.

✳

After dinner, after her brothers—who lived nearby, had a business fixing up old houses together, and still brought their laundry home—had left, her father carried her luggage down and fitted it into the car like pieces of a jigsaw puzzle. He had loved jigsaw puzzles, Susan recalled; when she was ten or so they'd spent long winter afternoons doing them, drinking hot chocolate with quiet pleasure. As they came in, she suggested they have some cocoa now. (At dinner she'd eaten nothing but the mashed potatoes.) Her mother fussed at them for dirtying the pot she'd just scrubbed and sent them into the living room. Susan settled on the carpet in front of the fire, enjoying the old sensation of heat on one cheek and the untraceable draft of cold air on the other. Her father talked about his time in San Diego during World War II and how he'd been sure California was full of promise. I'll have him visit, she told herself, after the baby . . . She drained the sweet silt at the bottom of her cup and her father said, "You're looking very pretty," and hummed a bit, *A pretty girl is like a melody*, the song he used to sing when she came downstairs dressed to go to a dance or party. Her mother would immediately find some detail amiss—a thread loose, slip showing, the hopeless unsymmetrical wave of her hair. One afternoon, just before she married, her husband-to-be had said, "Doesn't she look great?" and her mother answered, "That skirt does disguise your bottom." And Susan had taken that as praise.

Her mother came in to take the cups away. Susan noticed—now she would always notice—those blue-white weary circles, the way her lipstick had worn into tiny crevices.

And her secret gave her power.

"I want to take the dolls," she told her mother.

"The dolls?"

"The Barbies. I would like to take them with me. You'll never ship them for fear they'd get lost. So let me take them. They are mine?"

"Of course." Her mother had to say, "Of course." And she went into a fury of packing. She decided it wouldn't do to have them travel dressed—the clothes would rumple—so she stripped each one and laid the clothes out on Susan's bedspread. Each doll she tagged with her year and a clue to her outfit, rolled in tissue, and put into a large shopping bag. The Barbies weren't as interesting, Susan saw, as the outfits. Arrayed on the bed, they were something new, a work of art or anthropology. Their lines so sharp, their details so exacting, as if her mother had been sewing herself into the moment. They represented her mother's strenuous vision of perfection.

"They're beautiful," she told her mother.

"You'll probably get them all mixed up," she snapped.

Her mother put each set of clothes into a Baggie. "Be sure to get them out of these as soon as you can," she said. "Plastic isn't good for fabric. And *wash* them. When textiles get dirt in them, they rot." Susan nodded all through a lecture on soaking and detergents and how to use an iron, aware that she was taking something important away from her mother. But she'll forgive me, she thought, when she knows about the baby.

They put the clothes into another shopping bag and Susan promised to watch them every second, to take them inside with her when she stayed in motels, to avoid strong light, or heat, or cold. She minds their going, Susan thought, so much more than mine.

৵

On the other side of Cumberland—West!—light flurries whirled around the car. Susan drove into West Virginia. At noon she stopped at a scenic overlook where nothing could be seen but snow. She had packed a cooler with bottled water and liverwurst sandwiches. She never liked liverwurst before, but now she craved its smoothness, its blend of fat and iron. Liverwurst on rye. She started the car, still chewing, and drove into more snow. On into Kentucky, it turned to rain. The car got stuffy. She rolled down the window and warm wet air blew in. She smelled mud. She flew to the rhythm of the car, the wipers, the occasional lurch of her stomach. The radio played static, signs whistled by. Who knew what time it was? She reached into the bag beside her, pulled a doll from its nest of tissue, held it in her hand. Thin, hard, light. She balanced it like a weapon and then flicked it out the window. She laughed. It must be hormones. Through late afternoon, early twilight, every hundred miles or so, she flung another Barbie into the rush of air. The night turned foggy, but she would make it all the way to the Mississippi before she paused. Inside her the baby whirred, translucence with a heartbeat.

And behind her the Barbies took root and grew tall, casting their beautiful shadows over the land.

ﻙ